Dedalus European C
General Editor: Mike M

CW00542717

Spirite

Théophile Gautier

Spirite
and
The Coffee Pot

translated with an introduction
and chronology
by Patrick Jenkins

Dedalus

Dedalus would like to thank the French Ministry of Foreign Affairs in Paris for its assistance in producing this translation.

Published in the UK by Dedalus Ltd, Langford Lodge, St Judith's Lane, Sawtry, Cambs, PE17 5XE

UK ISBN 1 873982 96 8

Distributed in Australia & New Zealand by Peribo Pty Ltd, 58 Beaumont Road, Mount Kuring-gai N.S.W. 2080

Distributed in Canada by Marginal Distribution, Unit 102, 277 George Street North, Peterborough, Ontario, KJ9 3G9

First published in France in 1831 & 1865
First published by Dedalus in 1995
Translation copyright © Dedalus 1995

Printed in Finland by Wsoy
Typeset by Datix International Limited, Bungay, Suffolk

ABOUT THE TRANSLATOR

Patrick Jenkins was born in South Wales in 1968.

He was educated at the Universities of Kent & Warwick and is now a professional translator living in North London.

CHRONOLOGY

1811   August 30, Pierre-Jules-Théophile Gautier is born in Tarbes.

1829   At this stage, Gautier is still interested in a career as an artist, though it is not long before he devotes himself to literature.

1830   February 25, Gautier dons his famous red waistcoat to attend the fight for the cause of Romanticism, the so-called 'bataille d'Hernani'.

1835   Publication of the first section of *Mademoiselle de Maupin*. The second half is published the following year. The preface to the novel represents Gautier's manifesto on aesthetic freedom.

1836   February, Gautier's relationship with Eugénie Fort begins.
November, Eugenie Fort gives birth to Théophile Gautier *fils*.

1838   The next two years see publication of a number of short stories and novellas including *Fortunio* and *La Morte Amoureuse*.

1841   The Paris Opéra stages *Giselle ou les Wilis*, for which Gautier wrote the libretto. The star of the show is Carlotta Grisi, who becomes a great inspiration to Gautier.

1844   Gautier begins his long-standing relationship with the singer Ernesta Grisi, Carlotta's sister.

1845   summer, Gautier meets Charles Baudelaire for the first time.
August, Ernesta Grisi gives birth to Judith Gautier.

1847   November, Ernesta Grisi gives birth to Estelle Gautier.

1849   October, Gautier begins a relationship with Marie Mattei.

1852 June, Gautier breaks with Marie Mattei.
Publication of a number of works, including *Arria Marcella*.

1856 Publication of *L'Art Moderne*.

1857 Baudelaire publishes *Les Fleurs du Mal* and dedicates the work to Gautier.
Publication of *Avatar* and *Jettatura*.

1861 October, Gautier goes to stay with Carlotta Grisi, near Geneva.

1864 September–October, Gautier stays with Carlotta Grisi for a second time.

1865 July–November, Gautier visits Carlotta Grisi once more. During this stay, he writes *Spirite*.

1866 Publication of *Spirite*.
Over the next five years, Gautier continues to travel extensively as he has done all his life.

1871 Gautier moves into Eugenie Fort's apartment in Versailles.

1872 October 23, Gautier dies.

BIBLIOGRAPHY

Gautier's Fiction

Théophile Gautier wrote a large body of prose fiction. This list is a selection of those works which arguably bear the greatest relevance to *The Coffee Pot* and *Spirite*. There is very little of Gautier's prose available in translation, so some of the works mentioned here are the French editions.

One of Cleopatra's Nights, and other fantastic romances, translated by Lafcadio Hearn, New York, Worthington Co., 1886
Spirite suivi de La Morte Amoureuse, Paris, Flammarion, 1970
Mademoiselle de Maupin, translated with an introduction by Joanna Richardson, London, Penguin Classics, 1981
Contes Fantastiques, Paris, José Corti, 1986

Secondary texts

The following articles and books are concerned either with the work of Théophile Gautier directly or else they focus on some of the major issues Gautier raises in *Spirite*, *The Coffee Pot* and his other prose fiction.

Articles

Charles BAUDELAIRE, *Théophile Gautier,* in *Baudelaire: oeuvres complètes,* Editions du Seuil, 1968, pp.458–469
Ross CHAMBERS, *Gautier et le complexe de Pygmalion,* in *R.H.L.F,* 1972 no.4, pp.641–658
Harry COCKERHAM, *Gautier: from hallucination to supernatural vision,* in *Yale French Studies,* 50, April 1974, pp.42–53
M. CROUZET, *Gautier et le probleme de créer,* in *R.H.L.F,* 1972 no.4, pp.659–687
Edna Selan EPSTEIN, *The entanglement of sexuality and*

esthetics in Gautier and Mallarmé, in Nineteenth century French Studies (Fredonia), 1, 1972, pp.5–20

Nori FORNASIER, Pulsions et fonctions de l'idéal dans les contes fantastiques de Gautier, in Bulletin de la société Théophile Gautier, 6, 1984, pp.73–82

R. GIRAUD, Gautier's dehumanization of art, in L'esprit créateur, 3, 1963, pp.3–9

Alain MONTANDON, La séduction de l'oeuvre d'art chez Théophile Gautier, in Gautier, l'art et l'artiste (pp.349–368), (Actes du colloque international, Université Paul Valéry), Montpellier, Université Paul Valéry, 1983

Marie-Claude SCHAPIRA, Le thème du mort-vivant dans l'oeuvre en prose, in Europe, no.601, mai 1979, pp.41–49

Anne UBERSFELD, Gautier ou le regard de Pygmalion, in Romantisme, 66, 1989, pp.51–59

Friedrich WOLFZETTEL, Das Romantische Motiv der Steinernen Frau bei Théophile Gautier, in Neuphilologische Mitteilungen (Helsinki), 72, 1976, pp.254–269

Books

Rita BENESCH, Le regard de Théophile Gautier, Zurich, Juris Druck und Verlag Zurich, 1969

Natalie DAVID-WEILL, Rêve de pierre: la quête de la femme chez Théophile Gautier, Geneva, Droz, 1989

Elizabeth GOLDSMITH, Writing the Female Voice, London, Pinter, 1989

Robert M. TORRANCE, Ideal and Spleen: The Crisis of Transcendent Vision in Romantic, Symbolist and Modern Poetry, New York, London, Garland, 1987

INTRODUCTION

The forgotten prose of Théophile Gautier

Théophile Gautier was born in 1811 in Tarbes in the South of France. During his lifetime he travelled widely and had a number of relationships with women, including a long-standing liaison with Ernesta Grisi, who was the mother of his children, and a long-standing infatuation with Ernesta's sister Carlotta. Gautier died in 1872, aged 61.

During his lifetime, he was one of the best known and most highly respected writers in France. To his contemporaries - writers like Charles Baudelaire and Victor Hugo – he was one of the country's finest literary figures. So much so that in 1857, Baudelaire dedicated his celebrated *Fleurs du Mal* to Gautier, describing him as a 'perfect magician' and an 'impeccable poet'.

Yet today, when Baudelaire and Hugo are household names, Gautier's reputation has faded into the shadows, especially in the English-speaking world. Some will be acquainted with Gautier's poetry despite its fall from favour. Few, however, will associate his name with prose.

Nonetheless, Théophile Gautier produced a great deal of prose: travel writing, art and literary criticism. His great prose passion, though, was fantastical literature, and his fascination with it lasted his whole life. In 1831 he published his first fantastical tale, *The Coffee Pot* and in 1865 he published his last, the novella *Spirite*.

Gautier and the erotic fantastic

The fashion for the Gothic novel amongst English-speaking writers during the 18th and 19th centuries coincided with the popularity of 'the fantastic' and 'the marvellous' which embraced France and Germany in the 19th century. In many

11

ways the genre developed harmoniously in the two countries. So, for example, E.T.A. Hoffmann's technique of interweaving natural and supernatural in a 'marvellous' way proved a particularly powerful influence on Gautier. This said, a number of more personally specific trademarks clearly distinguish the Frenchman's brand of the fantastic from that of his contemporaries.

It is striking, for example, how much importance Gautier attaches to a character's eyes. Fantastical qualities underpin their often symbolic role throughout his *oeuvre*. The gaze is a window on the soul; the eye has supernatural power, or erotic, even phallic, significance; the eye of the body is separate from the eye of the soul. Dreaming is another vital theme. Whether awake or asleep, whether natural or drug-induced, it becomes a way of gaining access to a fantastical world.

Erotic desire is at the root of the eye fixation and the dreamy fantasy, as well as other fantastical themes and images that crop up regularly in Gautier's fiction. The erotic focus is a statue, a painting, a corpse, a spirit even, and it is so rarely discovered in the real world of living people that the desire itself is impossible to satisfy in the context of reality. There is an almost perpetual dichotomy between the physical perfection of an inanimate object of desire and the longing for interaction with that fantasy. So, a dead woman returns a kiss, a statue comes to life, a coffee pot becomes a flagrant mistress and a bodiless spirit tries to entice a man to love her.

Such scenarios have led to much critical study of the so-called Pygmalion complex in Gautier. Ovid portrayed Pygmalion as a sculptor who was able to recreate in ivory his ideal of female beauty. The statue was then brought to life by Venus to provide the sculptor with the incarnation of his ideal. So, it is argued, the hero of Gautier's fiction is Pygmalion in both respects: because he conceives of his ideal beauty in statuesque form and because his fantasy almost always desires that this inanimate icon of beauty should come to life.

But Gautier's version of the Pygmalion scenario is more complex than its mythical predecessor. Unlike the Roman

12

poet's version of the story, Gautier's tales present an icon of beauty that must retain her capacity to be inanimate even after she is brought to life. If she will not reassume her state of lifelessness, the hero feels threatened by the strong female that he paradoxically desires. One might have thought that a fantasy world would offer a chance for blissful happiness to a man who dreams of perfect beauty and longs to be led astray by a strong woman. But the safety mechanism of that fantasy, which saves the hero from a dangerous position of sub-ordination by arresting life from the object of desire, is what ultimately precludes him from attaining any such happiness. The erotic demand to be seduced by a perfect beauty, and yet always to be safe with her, seems to be too much of a contradiction for Gautier's hero.

From *The Coffee Pot* to *Spirite*

The chronological development of Théophile Gautier's fiction has long been the subject of critical attention. Many critics have put forward a simplistic linear progression theory, arguing that early works are materialistic and late works spiritualistic. A superficial look at the two texts in this collection, *The Coffee Pot* (1831) and Gautier's last major work of fiction, *Spirite* (1866), tends to reinforce this viewpoint.

Mademoiselle de Maupin (1835), one of the better known examples of Gautier's early fiction, seems to concentrate on the physical appearance of things and on a sensual response to beauty.

The title of *Spirite* suggests a concern with the spiritual side of things and this is certainly the obvious focus of the text.

Despite appearances, however, a fascination with both physical and spiritual beauty runs through all of Gautier's texts.

Although the reader of *The Coffee Pot* is introduced to an erotic beauty, her eyes are so transparent the narrator can see through to her soul. And later, when he sits entwined with his love, his soul 'is released from its prison of mud to float in ethereal infinity'. In *Spirite*, on the other hand, when the

13

subjects are two souls already free of the material constraints of the human body, they float away, but as they do so, they fly next to one another 'in a state of heavenly, radiant bliss, caressing each other with the tips of their wings and fondling each other with divinely provocative gestures.'

Anything more than a cursory examination of Gautier's fiction reveals a startling consistency through virtually every text, regardless of when it was written. There is always an aesthetic appreciation of beauty and an erotic fixation with physical form; and yet the response to that form is almost invariably expressed in spiritual terms of some sort.

Besides reflecting the underlying balance between physical and spiritual in Gautier's work, the two texts in this collection also illustrate another much neglected aspect of his writing. As well as displaying a consuming interest in beauty, the stories can also be great fun. *The Coffee Pot*, with its wonderfully pictorial descriptions, is a perfect illustration. The central animated scene, in particular, shows off the author's penchant for comic fantasy. By contrast, *Spirite* exemplifies the wry side of Gautier's sense of humour. And though the wit is less obvious, it is perhaps more interesting, since it forms part of a commentary on the social rites and fashions of the day. Despite this, the work has not dated: much of the social comment in *Spirite* is as true of Western society today as it was of Gautier's Paris. So while *Spirite* might initially seem further removed from the realities of this world than any of Gautier's earlier texts – because one of its main characters is a bodiless soul – it does actually provide a very clear insight into the workings of society.

For today's reader, one of the most interesting and striking facets of this social comment is Gautier's apparent fascination with the position of women in the world. The eponymous heroine of *Spirite* uses her position as a soul that has lived on earth to give the reader a posthumous insight into a woman's miserable destiny:

> The lot of women is such a harrowing one [. . .],
> condemned to waiting, inaction and silence. They

14

cannot show their preferences without losing their image of propriety. They must endure the love they inspire and they must never declare the love they feel.

Although *The Coffee Pot* ends before *its* heroine gets the chance to bemoan her tragic fate, this does not mean that Gautier's early texts display an insensitivity to the discrimination women suffer(ed) in society. In *Mademoiselle de Maupin*, Madeleine revolts against the stereotype of dainty womanhood and declares: '. . . it bores me to speak in a little, fluty, honey-sweet voice. [. . .] The thing I dislike most in the world is obeying orders.' Whether this represents a disinterested promotion of woman's liberation, or whether Gautier's narrators and heroes just have an erotic fantasy about strong, liberated women, is another matter. The motives seem all the more questionable since *Mademoiselle de Maupin* also broaches the theme of lesbianism: is this really a plea for women's rights or just a voyeuristic fantasy?

There are a number of reasons for bringing *The Coffee Pot* and *Spirite* together in this collection. Perhaps most importantly they are Gautier's first and last fantastical tales. And as such they show some of the consistencies and evolutions that occur through his *oeuvre* as a whole. But *Spirite* is also a neat sequel to *The Coffee Pot* because together the two texts chart the course of a male erotic fantasy. The narrator of *The Coffee Pot* ends his tale with the words, 'I realised then that there was no happiness left for me on earth'. And it is *Spirite*'s Guy de Malivert who seems to pursue the idea as he experiences the temptation of striking up a relationship with a soul that is no longer of this earth.

THE COFFEE POT

I saw through sombre veil
Eleven stars, sun and moon all pale.
In silence deep
And reverentially
They pay me
Homage all through my sleep.

Joseph's Vision.

I

Last year I was invited, together with two artist friends of mine, Arrigo Cohic and Pedrino Borgnioli, to spend a few days on an estate in southern Normandy.

The fickle weather, which had seemed extremely promising when we set off, suddenly changed and it rained so heavily that the hollowed out tracks we were walking on became more like the bed of a torrential river.

We were sinking into sludge up to our knees and a thick layer of slimy earth had attached itself to the soles of our boots, its weight slowing our progress so much that we did not arrive at our destination until an hour after sunset.

We were exhausted and our host could see that we were straining to contain our yawns and keep our eyes open, so as soon as we had had supper, he led each of us to our own room.

Mine was vast. Walking into it, a kind of feverish chill ran down my spine; it was as though I was entering a new world. To see Boucher's representation of the four seasons above the doors, the furniture overladen with rococo ornamentation in the worst possible taste, and the heavy sculpture of the mirrored panels, one might actually have thought oneself in Regency France.

Nothing had been done to clear things away. The dressing table, covered with boxes of combs and powder puffs, seemed to have been used just the day before. Two or three dresses which changed colour in the light and a fan studded with silver sequins were strewn over the well-waxed floor. And to my great astonishment, an enamel snuffbox lay open in the hearth, full of still fresh tobacco.

I did not notice these things until after the servant had placed his candlestick on the bedside table and bid me good-night; then, I swear, I began to tremble like a leaf. I undressed swiftly, got into bed and, to put an end to my foolish fears, quickly shut my eyes and turned towards the wall. But I found it impossible to stay in this position: the bed was tossing beneath me like the sea and my eyelids were being forced open. I felt compelled to turn around and look.

The flaming fire was casting a reddish light across the apartment so that it was easy to make out the characters of the tapestry and the faces of the smoky portraits which hung on the wall. They were our host's ancestors, knights in armour, wigged counsellors and beautiful ladies with painted faces, white powdered hair and a rose in one hand.

Suddenly the fire began to flicker strangely; a pale light illuminated the room and I saw clearly that what I had assumed were merely paintings were in fact reality; the eyes of these framed individuals shifted and shone in a remarkable way; their lips moved like the lips of people talking but I could hear nothing except the tick-tock of the clock and the whistle of the autumnal North wind.

An overwhelming terror gripped me, my hair bristled on my forehead, my teeth chattered so violently I thought they would shatter and a cold sweat soaked my whole body.

The clock struck eleven. The vibration of the last chime resounded for a long time and when it had completely died away. . .

No, I dare not say what happened. No one would believe me; people would think I was mad.

The candles lit themselves; unaided by any visible force, the bellows began to fan the fire, rattling like an asthmatic old man; the tongs poked about in the embers and the shovel gathered up the cinders. Then a coffee pot threw itself down from a table on which it had been standing and hobbled over to the hearth, where it settled itself amongst the embers. A few moments later the armchairs set off and with their cork-screw feet flitting around in an astonishing way they came and gathered around the fireplace.

II

I did not know what to think of what I was seeing; but much more extraordinary things were yet to happen.

One of the portraits, the oldest of the lot, was of a big round-faced man with a grey beard, who looked just as I had imagined Sir John Falstaff to look. Grimacing, this man's head freed itself from its frame. Then with a great deal of effort he squeezed his shoulders and pot-belly between the narrow strips of the border before jumping heavily on to the floor.

He had no sooner caught his breath than he pulled a peculiarly small key from his waistcoat pocket, blew on it to make sure the bit was cleanly cut and then unlocked each of the frames one after another. Whereupon all the frames expanded to let out the pictures they contained.

Chubby little priests, dry sallow dowagers, serious-looking magistrates shrouded in great black robes, dandies in silk stockings and dark woollen breeches, holding the points of their swords up high: all these characters created such a strange spectacle that despite my fear, I could not help laughing. And these worthy characters seated themselves; and the coffee pot jumped lightly up on to the table. They drank their coffee from blue and white Japanese cups, which came running along spontaneously from on top of a writing desk, each one accompanied by a lump of sugar and a small silver spoon.

When the coffee was finished, coffee pot, cups and spoons all disappeared together and a conversation started up that was certainly the most curious I have ever witnessed: none of these strange characters looked at one another as they con-

21

versed but instead kept staring at the clock. I too was unable to take my eyes off it or stop following the hands as they marched imperceptibly on to midnight.

Finally midnight struck and a voice with exactly the same tone as the clock could be heard saying:

'The time has come; you must dance.'

The company rose. The chairs moved back of their own accord and each knight took a lady by the hand. Then the same voice said:

'Members of the orchestra, let the music commence!'

I have omitted to mention that one half of the tapestry portrayed an Italian orchestra and the other half, a stag hunt with some whips blowing hunting horns. The whips and the musicians, who had not moved a muscle until now, inclined their heads as a sign of mutual under-standing.

The maestro raised his baton and a lively, dancing melody started up on either side of the room. The first dance was a minuet. But the quick notes of the score the musicians were playing clashed with the sober bows and curtsies of the dance, so after a few minutes all the couples began to pirou-ette like German spinning tops. The women's silk dresses, ruffled by this dancing whirlwind, made peculiar sounds just like the flapping wings of a flock of pigeons. And the wind surging beneath the dresses puffed them out prodigously, making them look like swinging bells.

The virtuosos' bows moved so fast on the strings that elec-tric sparks flew. The flautists' fingers rose and fell like quicksil-ver; the hornblowers' cheeks were inflated like balloons. And all this created such a hurried deluge of notes and trills, such an incredible torrent of ascending and descending scales that all hell would not have been able to keep up such a speed for even two minutes.

It was pitiful too to see the efforts of those dancers, as they tried to keep pace. They jumped, cavorted, twirled and bounded and leapt three feet into the air; so energetic were they that the sweat ran down their brows and into their eyes and washed off their beauty spots and their make-up. Try as they might, however, the orchestra was always three or four notes ahead of them.

The clock struck one. They stopped. And I saw something which had escaped my notice: a woman who had not been dancing.

She was sitting in a Queen Anne armchair in a corner by the fireplace and seemed to be totally isolated from what was going on around her.

Never, even in my dreams, have my eyes been presented with anything so perfect: her skin was a dazzling white, her hair was ash blond; she had long eyelashes and blue eyes, so clear and transparent that I could see through to her soul as distinctly as one might see a pebble on the bed of a stream. And I felt that if ever I should love anyone, it would be her. I leapt out of bed, where I had been rooted until now and I moved towards her, unconsciously driven by something controlling me from within. Then I found myself at her knees, with one of her hands in mine, chatting away as though I had known her for twenty years.

But as I was talking to her, my head was rocking in time to the continuing music, in a strange and wonderful way; and although I was overjoyed to be in conversation with such a beautiful person, my feet were burning to dance with her.

However, I did not dare ask her. She seemed to understand what I wanted for she raised the hand I was not holding towards the clock face and said:

'When the hand gets to there we shall see, my dear Théodore.'

I do not know how she knew my name but I was not in the least surprised to hear her call me by it, and we continued our chat. Finally, when the clock struck the time she had said, the voice with the silvery tone resonated again throughout the room, with the words:

'Angéla, you can dance with the gentleman if it will make you happy, but you know what will happen.'

'I don't care,' Angéla replied sulkily, and passed her ivory arm around my neck.

'Prestissimo,' cried the voice. And we began to waltz. The

girl's breast was against my chest, her velvet cheek brushed my own and her sweet breath hung on my lips.

Never in my life have I experienced an emotion like it: my nerves were on tenterhooks, blood was flowing through my arteries like torrents of lava and I could hear my heart beat as though it were strapped to my ears. Not that it was an unpleasant state to be in. I was flooded with a feeling of ineffable joy and I wanted it to stay that way for ever. The orchestra was playing at triple speed now but remarkably we did not need to make any effort to keep pace.

Everyone present, amazed by our agility, was shouting bravo and clapping with all their might, though their hands made no sound.

Until now Angéla had waltzed with astonishing energy and precision but suddenly she seemed to tire; she leant on my shoulder as though she had no legs of her own; her tiny feet which had been skimming over the floor just moments earlier, could now only drag themselves from its surface, as if they were weighed down with lead.

'Angéla,' I said to her, 'you're weary. Let's rest.'

'I'd like to,' she replied, wiping her brow with her handkerchief, 'but while we've been waltzing everyone else has sat down: there's only one chair left and there are two of us.'

'What does that matter, my beautiful angel? You can sit on my knee.'

III

Without the slightest objection, Angéla sat down, wrapping her arms around me like a white scarf and burying her head in my breast to warm herself a little: she had gone as cold as marble.

I do not know how long we stayed in this position because all my senses were absorbed in the contemplation of this mysterious and fantastic creature. I no longer had any concept of time or space; the real world no longer existed for me and all links with it were broken; my soul was released from its prison of mud to float in ethereal infinity. I understood what no mortal can understand: Angéla did not have to say a word for her thoughts to be clear to me; her soul shone inside her body like an alabaster lamp and the rays emitted from her heart passed right through my own.

The lark sang. A pale light played on the curtains. And as soon as Angéla saw this, she got hurriedly to her feet and gestured farewell to me. After a few steps she cried out and fell headlong. Seized with fright, I rushed over to help her to her feet. . . My blood runs cold just thinking about it. All I found was the coffee pot shattered into a thousand pieces.

Seeing this, and being convinced that I had been the plaything of some diabolical illusion, I was overcome by such a sense of fear that I fainted.

IV

When I regained consciousness, I was in my bed with Arrigo Cohic and Pedrino Borgnioli at my side.

As soon as I had opened my eyes, Arrigo cried out:

'And about time too. I've been rubbing your temples with eau-de-Cologne for nearly an hour. What the devil were you doing last night? I noticed that you hadn't come down this morning so I came into your room and there you were, stretched right out on the floor, wearing some old-fashioned French clothes and clutching a piece of broken porcelain in your arms as though it were some pretty girl.'

'Good Lord, it's my grandfather's wedding suit,' said my other friend, lifting up one of the pink silk coat tails, with its green leaf patterning. 'And there are the paste buttons with their tracery decoration which he told us so much about. Théodore must have found it all tucked away in a corner and put it on for the fun of it. What was it that made you faint, though?' Borgnioli added. 'Fainting is fine when it happens to a white-shouldered little wench: you unlace her bodice, take off her necklaces and her scarf and it's a wonderful opportunity to start seducing her.'

'I was just overcome by weakness: I'm prone to that sort of thing,' I replied dryly.

I stood up and got rid of my ridiculous outfit. And then we had lunch. My friends ate a lot and drank even more. I, however, ate almost nothing, being strangely preoccupied with the memory of what had happened.

When lunch was over, we could not go out because of the heavy rain, so we occupied ourselves as best we could. Borgnioli drummed his fingers in warlike marches on the window panes and Arrigo and our host played draughts. I, meanwhile, took a square of vellum from my pad and began to draw.

Though I would never have dreamt it, the almost imperceptible outlines traced by my pencil actually represented, with the most amazing accuracy, the coffee pot which had played such an important role in the scenes of the night.

'It's astonishing how much that head looks like my sister Angéla,' said our host, who, having finished his game, was watching over my shoulder as I worked.

And in fact what had seemed to me a moment earlier to be a coffee pot, was really and truly Angéla's sweet and melancholic profile.

'In heaven's name, is she dead or alive?' I cried out, my voice trembling as though my life depended on his reply.

'She died two years ago after catching pneumonia at a ball.'

'God, no!' I replied in anguish.

Holding back a tear which was on the verge of falling, I replaced the sheet of paper in the pad.

I realised then that there was no happiness left for me on earth.

SPIRITE

CHAPTER 1

Guy de Malivert was stretched out, virtually sitting on his shoulders, in a superb armchair near his hearth, where a good fire was burning. He seemed to have settled down for a quiet evening at home; one of those evenings which become both a delight and a necessity for today's fashionable young people who from time to time find themselves exhausted by society's pleasures. He wore a black velvet jacket embellished with black silk patches, a cotton shirt, trousers with red flannel bottoms and big Moroccan slippers in which his arched feet twitched: his outfit was comfortable but elegant. His body felt free of all constricting pressure and at ease in this soft and supple clothing. Guy de Malivert had stayed at home to enjoy a meal of studied simplicity, enlivened by two or three glasses of excellent Bordeaux that had been to India and back, and now he was experiencing the kind of physical bliss which comes about when the various parts of the body are in perfect accord. He was happy without anything wonderful having happened to him.

Near him, a lamp, fitted inside a cornet-shape of old crackled celadon, cast a milky glow from its frosted glass cover that was like moonbeams seen through a mist. The light fell on to a copy of Longfellow's *Evangeline*, which Guy was holding loosely in one hand.

Guy no doubt admired the work of the greatest poet that the young land of America has ever produced, but his soul was in that lazy state when an absence of thought is preferable to the most beautiful idea, however sublime the terms in which it may be expressed. He had read several lines when, without releasing the book, he had leant his head on the soft guipure-covered padding of the chair and begun quite contentedly letting his mind empty itself of thought. The warm air of the room enveloped him in its sweet caress. Around him all was tranquillity, well-being, discreet silence and intimate quiet. The only perceptible sound was the whistle of a jet of gas coming from a log and the tick-tock of the clock as the pendulum recorded the passing of time in a hushed voice.

It was winter. The freshly fallen snow dulled the distant drone of carriages, which were quite rare in this deserted neighbourhood, as Guy lived in one of the least busy streets of the district of Saint-Germain. Ten o'clock had just struck and our lazy hero was congratulating himself on not being at some embassy ball or other, standing in a window recess, wearing a black suit and a white tie, and having nothing else to look at but the boney shoulder-blades of an old dowager in a ridiculously low-cut dress. Although the prevailing temperature in the room was reminiscent of a greenhouse, the ardour of the burning fire and the profound silence of the streets were enough to make one realise it was cold outside. The magnificent angora cat, Malivert's companion on this idle evening, had moved closer to the hearth to tan its white fur and it was only the gilt fire-guard which prevented it actually lying amongst the embers.

The room in which Guy de Malivert was sampling these peaceful delights was midway between the study and the studio. It was a vast high-ceilinged room on the top floor of the house in which Guy lived; it ran from front to back, overlooking on one side a great courtyard, and on the other a garden planted with the kind of age-old trees that are worthy of a royal forest, the type of garden which only the suburban aristocracy possess nowadays: it takes time to produce a tree and today's nouveau riche are unable to use trees to shade their mansions because they build them in such a hurry and with a fortune that is threatened by bankruptcy.

The walls were covered with beige leather and the ceiling was made up of intersecting beams of mature oak, framing coffers of Norwegian pine, whose natural colour had been left unstained. The sober brown tones of the decor enhanced the effect of the paintings, sketches and watercolours which hung on the walls of this makeshift gallery where Malivert had gathered his collection of artistic curiosities and fantasies.

Oak bookcases, not so tall as to spoil the pictures, gave the impression of a sort of lower storey around the room, interrupted by just one door. The books displayed on these shelves would have surprised the observer, so varied was their subject matter. In fact, one might easily have assumed this room to be the shared library of an artist and a scholar. Alongside the classical poets of every age and every country – Homer, Hesiod, Virgil, Dante, Ariosto, Ronsard, Shakespeare, Milton, Goethe, Schiller, Lord Byron, Victor Hugo, Sainte-Beuve, Alfred de Musset and Edgar Allan Poe – there resided Creuzer's *Symbolik*, Laplace's *Mécanique Céleste*, Arago's *Astronomie*, Burdach's *Physiologie* and Humboldt's *Kosmos*, as well as the works of Claude Bernard and Berthelot and other studies of the pure sciences. Yet Guy de Malivert was not an academic. He had barely learnt what one is taught at school but, after educating himself in literature, he had thought it shameful to know nothing of the fine scientific discoveries which glorified his own century. He had done his best to keep abreast of things and felt quite at home listening to someone talk about astronomy, cosmogony, electricity, gases, photography, chemistry, micrography, or spontaneous generation: he understood what was being said and would sometimes astonish his company by making an ingenious and original remark himself.

This was Guy de Malivert at 28 or 29 years of age. His full-lipped mouth, shaded by a moustache of reddish gold, suggested a kind heart; his nose, although not of the classical Greek variety, was certainly not lacking in nobility; it separated two stern brown eyes. His hair, thinning a little on the top of his head, gave him a frank, open and pleasant expression; it was a warm shade of brown and such a mass of tiny kinks and curls that it had always resisted the barber's hair iron. Basically, Malivert was what people call a good-looking chap, and when he entered society, he met with considerable success without actively seeking it out. Mothers with daughters to marry off fussed over him, for he had an income of 40,000 francs a year from the land he owned, and a doddering, multi-millionaire for an uncle, from whom he would

31

inherit. An admirable position indeed! Yet Guy had not married. When a young lady performed a sonata before him, he would just nod his approval. At a ball, he would accompany his partner politely back to her seat after the contra-dance, but during the breaks between dances his conversation was restricted to such phrases as, 'It really is warm in this room' an aphorism from which it is impossible to deduce the slightest matrimonial intention. Not that Guy de Malivert lacked wit; he could easily have found something less banal to say if he had not been worried about getting caught up in the kind of web woven of a thread more subtle than a spider's web; the kind of web that surrounds every nubile virgin of the world with a small dowry.

Whenever he realised that he was abnormally welcome in a home, he stopped going there; or he went away on a journey and when he came back he had the satisfaction of seeing himself totally forgotten. You might think that Guy, like many young people today, indulged in brief morganatic relationships with the demi-monde which made actual marriage unnecessary. That, however, was far from true. While he avoided being more austere than befitted his years, Malivert was not drawn to these beauties who plaster themselves with make-up, have hairstyles like poodles and puff out their frocks with excessive crinoline underskirts. That was just not his style. Like everyone else, he had had his fair share of good fortune. Two or three frustrated women, who had more or less separated from their husbands, had declared him their ideal, to which he had replied, 'You are very kind', not daring to tell them that they were far from being *his* ideal: Malivert was a well brought-up fellow, after all. An unsuccessful actress from the Délassements-Comiques, to whom he had given money and a velvet cape, had claimed he had betrayed her and had tried to suffocate herself because of it; but despite these wonderful adventures, Guy de Malivert was true to himself and realised that having reached the solemn age of 29, when a youth is on the verge of becoming a young man, he still knew nothing of love, as it is portrayed in the poems, plays and novels he read or even as it was described to him by friends who confided in him or others who boasted to him. He consoled himself quite easily in his misfortune, by imagining the worries, the troubles and the disaster to which this passion could lead; he awaited the day with patience, when some decisive object of desire would appear by chance and make him settle down.

Nevertheless, since the world so often treats a man according to its own will and convenience, it had been decided within the circles which Guy tended to frequent, that he was in love with Madame d'Ymbercourt, a young widow whom he visited quite regularly. Madame d'Ymbercourt's estate was adjacent to Guy's; and from it, she earned about 60,000 francs in revenue, though she was only 22 years old. Rather conveniently Monsieur d'Ymbercourt, her sullen old husband, had passed away leaving her in a position to marry an attractive young man whose breeding and fortune equalled her own. Society had thus taken it upon itself to marry them off, thinking that the couple's new home would be pleasant, neutral ground on which to meet. Madame d'Ymbercourt tacitly accepted this marriage and in many ways already perceived herself as Guy's wife; he, meanwhile, was far from eager to make a declaration of love and was in fact considering ceasing his visits to the home of the pretty widow, whose presumptuous desire to trap him into marriage he found slightly tedious.

This same evening, Guy was invited for tea at Madame d'Ymbercourt's. But after dinner, indolence had taken hold of him and he had felt so contented in his own home that he recoiled at the prospect of dressing and going out into a bitterly cold evening despite his fur-lined coat and the hot-water bottle in his carriage. As a pretext, he had told himself that his horse was not shod for icy conditions and that it might well slip dangerously on the hardened snow. In actual fact, he was not at all worried about leaving his horse outside Madame d'Ymbercourt's house for two or three hours: he had after all paid Crémieux, the famous horse-trader on the Champs-Elysées, 5,000 francs for the animal, so it should be able to withstand a North wind. Clearly Guy was not particularly in love and Madame d'Ymbercourt was going to have to wait a long time for the ceremony which would allow her to change her name.

All the while, Malivert sat amidst a blueish smoke which wafted from two or three cabaña cigars. The cigar ash filled a small cup of antique Chinese bronze with an eagle-wood base, which was placed next to a lamp on a small trestle-table beside him. Lulled by the sweet warmth of the room, Guy was beginning to feel the first grains of the gold dust of sleep being sprinkled beneath his eyelids when the door to his room opened cautiously and his servant appeared carrying a dainty perfumed letter on a silver tray. Guy knew the seal only too well and his expression turned instantly to one of ill humour. The smell of musk from the paper also seemed to affect him disagreeably. It was a note from Madame d'Ymbercourt reminding him of his promise to visit her for tea.

'Damn her and her little notes,' he shouted. 'They give me such a headache.' His outburst was a little discourteous, it must be said. 'What fun it would be to go right to the other side of town, just to drink a cup of warm water, in which she has marinaded a few grey-green or Prussian blue leaves. In this Coromandel lacquered box I have tea from the Orient, authentic tea, clearly marked with a customs stamp from Kiatka, the last Russian outpost on the Chinese border. No, I definitely won't be going.'

A vague residue of politeness made him change his mind. He told his manservant to bring his clothes. But when he saw the legs of his trousers hanging pathetically on the back of the chair, the stiff white shirt like a piece of porcelain, the black jacket with its dangling arms, the polished boots with their gleaming reflections and the long gloves like hands that had gone through a mangle, a feeling of despair suddenly enveloped him and he quickly snuggled down into his chair.

'I'm definitely staying at home. Jack, go and prepare my bed.'

As we have already established, Guy had been well brought up but more than that, he had a good heart. Moved

34

by a slight feeling of remorse, he hesitated on the threshold of his bedroom, as it beckoned him with all its intimate comforts. He decided that even the most basic politeness demanded he send word of apology to Madame d'Ymbercourt; he could claim he had a migraine, an important meeting, or some trouble or other that had just come up as he was leaving – anything that would allow him to cry off decently. Though Malivert was not a writer by profession, he was quite capable of producing some travel writing or a short story for the *Revue des Deux Mondes* but he did hate writing letters, especially this kind of note which women scribble by the dozen purely for reasons of etiquette. They write them at the corner of their washstand while they are dressed by their maids, Clotilde or Rose. He would have preferred to write a sonnet on rare and difficult rhymes. He was so unable to write this kind of letter that he would sometimes go in person from one side of town to the other, just to avoid producing a two-line note. It was the fear of writing a note now, that made Guy consider once more the desperate idea of going to see Madame d'Ymbercourt. He walked to the window and half opened the curtains; through the window panes, damp with condensation, he could see a black night, so densely speckled with little flakes of white that it looked like a guinea-fowl's back. This made him think of Grymalkin, shaking the covering of snow from its shining coat. He imagined the unpleasant walk between the coupé and the foyer, and the draughty stairway, which the heating could do nothing to rectify; above all, he thought of Madame d'Ymbercourt standing against the mantelpiece, wearing her finest clothes; her dress would be so low-cut that she brought to mind the Dickens character who is always referred to as 'The Bosom' and whose expanse of white flesh is ample enough to allow a banker to display his prospectus of wealth on it; he saw her superb teeth, framed by a fixed smile; her eyebrows, shaped in such a perfect arc that one might have thought them drawn on with Indian ink, but which in fact owed nothing to art; her magnificent eyes; her nose so perfect it would have made the ideal model for a textbook on

35

form; her waist, proclaimed faultless by dressmakers everywhere; her arms, laden with oversized bracelets, and so well rounded they might have been sculpture; and the memory of all these charms, which society was granting him, as it married him off to the young widow, without his being particularly keen on the idea, inspired in him a melancholy so profound that he walked towards his desk, intent, awful as the prospect was, on penning ten lines rather than go to take tea with this charming woman.

He placed before him a sheet of off-white paper, embossed with a G and an M flamboyantly intertwined. He dipped into the ink the steel nib of a fine fountain pen, the top of which was made from the spine of a porcupine; and quite low down the page, to reduce the amount of space left for the actual literature, he wrote the triumphant word: 'Madame'. Then he paused and rested his cheek on the palm of his hand: his creative juices had dried up. For several minutes he remained with his wrist poised, his fingers extended down the length of the pen and his brain involuntarily wandering on to subjects which bore no relation to his letter. As if, while waiting for that elusive phrase, Malivert's body had lost patience, his hand was overcome with pins and needles; it began to fidget and seemed to want to get on with its task without awaiting instruction. The fingers straightened and clenched as though to form letters on the page. And to Guy's great surprise he discovered he had written nine or ten lines totally unconsciously. These he then read and their meaning was roughly this:

'You are beautiful enough and surrounded by enough admirers to permit someone to say, without causing you offence, that he does not love you. It is a black mark against the man who makes such an admission. So be it. What point is there in continuing a relationship, destined to result in two souls so little suited being united and bound together in eternal unhappiness? Forgive me but I am going away. I'm certain you will have no difficulty forgetting me.'

'What is this?' said Malivert, striking the table with his fist, when he had re-read the note. 'Am I mad or have I been writing in my sleep? This letter is bizarre to say the very least. It's like one of Gavarni's lithographs, with a caption relating both what someone has written and what he is thinking, the lies and the truth. Except here, the written word does not deceive. I had every intention of telling a white lie for the sake of etiquette but instead, and quite contrary to conventional practice, this letter conveys sincerity.'

Guy studied the note carefully and it seemed to him that the style of the writing was not quite his own. 'Granted, this may be a piece of my own handwritten prose but if ever my letters were deemed worthy of study, I'm sure this would be contested by the experts. How the devil can this strange transformation have come about? I haven't been smoking opium or eating hashish and I am sure those two or three glasses of Bordeaux cannot have gone to my head. My mind is sturdier than that. What will become of me if the truth comes flowing from my pen like that without my realising? Luckily I re-read my epistle – my spelling is never too accurate in the evenings. But imagine the effect these pleasant and all too truthful words would have caused and the indignation and stupefaction which would have crossed Madame d'Ymbercourt's face as she read them? Perhaps, though, it would have been better to send the letter as it was. I would have been taken for a monster, a tattooed savage unworthy of donning a white tie and tails but at least this tedious liaison would have been broken as cleanly as glass; and glass, after all, cannot be mended, even by patching it with paper. If I were a little superstitious I would be inclined to think the whole affair a warning from above, rather than some inexplicable lapse of concentration.'

After a pause Guy suddenly decided on a drastic course of action: 'I'm quite unable to rewrite this letter, so I shall go to Madame d'Ymbercourt's.' In angry mood, he dressed and was about to leave his room when he thought he heard someone sigh but it was so feeble, so faint, so ethereal a sigh, that the profound silence of the night was essential for the ear to perceive it. The sigh halted Malivert in the doorway of his study and affected him in the same way as any supernatural occurrence affects even the most courageous individual. There was nothing really frightening about this vague, inarticulate and plaintive cry and yet it troubled Guy more than he dared admit to himself.

'Oh, it must have been my cat whining in its sleep,' said Malivert, taking a fur coat from the hands of his manservant. Wrapping it around himself with the savoir faire of a man who has travelled extensively in Russia, he went down in a fairly foul mood to the front steps, where his carriage awaited him.

CHAPTER 2

Curled up in the corner of his carriage with his feet on his water bottle and his fur coat wrapped tightly around him, Malivert watched but saw nothing of the strange play of light and shade on the slightly misted-up window. Nor did he see the sudden bursts of illumination from little shops still ablaze with gas light and open even at this late hour; or the landscape of streets lit up by the occasional spot of brilliant, starry brightness.

The carriage soon crossed the Pont de la Concorde and beneath the bridge, the Seine flowed on through the darkness with its shimmering gloom and lantern reflections. During the journey, Malivert could not help thinking of the mysterious sigh he had heard, or thought he had heard, just as he left his room. He repeated to himself all the natural explanations for the incomprehensible that are put forward by sceptics. There was no doubt about it: it must have been the wind trapped in the chimney or in the corridor; the echo of some noise from outside, making it sound different; or one of the piano strings resonating after being disturbed by the passing of a heavy carriage. It might even have been his angora cat whining, as it lay dreaming in front of the fire, just as he had first imagined. Nothing was more likely, or more rational. Malivert recognised how logical these explanations were and yet deep down he felt them to be unsatisfactory; a secret instinct told him that sigh was not caused by anything to which his philosophical wisdom attributed it; he sensed that feeble moaning had issued from a soul, that it was not a vague material sound; there was breath and pain in it. Where then had it come from? Guy only considered this question with the kind of questioning anxiety which the sturdiest of minds experiences, the sort of mind that encounters the unknown without seeking it out. There had been no one in the room, no one except Jack, and Jack is no sentimentalist; the sigh was sweetly warbled, harmonious and tender, and gentler than a whispering breeze through aspen leaves. It was undoubtedly feminine; this aspect of its character could not be denied.

Another detail which intrigued Malivert was that letter which had written itself, as it were, as though some will other than his own had guided his fingers. Guy had initially fooled himself that it had been a lapse of concentration but this excuse could hardly be taken seriously. The soul's sentiments are checked over by the mind before being committed to paper; and besides, they are not going to compose themselves into a letter while the brain is dreaming of something else. Some guiding force he could not define must have taken hold of him while he was absent from his own self and then acted in his stead, for he was quite sure, now that he thought about it, that he had not slept for a single moment; all evening he had felt lazy, drowsy and numbed by a languorous sense of well-being, but at the moment in question he had been perfectly awake.

The tiresome alternatives of going to see Madame d'Ymbercourt or writing her a note declining the invitation had even aroused in him a certain feverish overexcitement. These lines had captured his secret thoughts so exactly and more precisely than he had yet admitted to himself; they were the product of an interventionist force that would simply have to be called supernatural, until analysis explained it or gave it another name.

As Guy de Malivert went over these questions in his head, the carriage rolled on through the streets. The cold and the snow meant they were more deserted than those in the elegant and wealthy parts of the city, where night life goes on until very late. Place de la Concorde, Rue de Rivoli, Place Vendo[lc]me, were soon left behind, and the coupé went along the boulevard before turning the corner into Rue de la Chausée-d'Antin, where Madame d'Ymbercourt lived.

As he entered the courtyard, Guy experienced an unpleasant sensation: two lines of carriages, their coachmen bound up in furs, were parking in the sandy area which occupied the centre of the courtyard; the horses were shaking their bits and sending a shower of froth on to the cobbles to mix with the flakes of snow.

'This is what she calls an intimate evening; this is her idea of a cup of tea around the fire. It's the only kind of evening she ever has. The whole of Paris will be there,' muttered Malivert, 'and here am I with no white tie. I'd have been better off going to bed, but I tried to be a diplomat like Talleyrand; I didn't want to follow my first instinct because that was the right one.'

He climbed the steps slowly and, after freeing himself of his fur coat, he headed for the drawing room. A servant opened the doors for him with a kind of deference that was both obsequious and conspiratorial, as though to a man who would soon be the master of the house and in whose service he would like to remain.

'What is going on?' said Guy de Malivert to himself in a low voice, noticing that this servility was more accentuated than usual. 'It's not the servants' place to take care of me and give their personal blessing to my marrying Madame d'Ymbercourt! The wedding hasn't been announced yet, anyway.'

Guy approached Madame d'Ymbercourt with his head lowered and his back arched, which is the modern way to greet someone. When Madame d'Ymbercourt noticed him she gave a little squeal of contentment, which she tried to correct with an air of sulky coldness. But her ever-smiling lips, used to revealing her impeccable pearly teeth right to their pink gums, could not come together to put on the pretty pout that was called for. Out of the corner of one eye, the lady could see in a mirror that this expression was not a success, and so she resolved to play the good little girl, like an indulgent woman who knows that these days one must not demand much of male gallantry.

'How late you are, Monsieur Guy,' she said, holding out to him a tiny hand so tightly gloved that it seemed wooden to the touch. 'No doubt you've been hanging around at that horrible club of yours, smoking your cigars and shuffling

41

cards. Your punishment is that you missed hearing Kreisler, the great German pianist, playing Listz's *Grand Chromatic Gallop*, and the lovely countess Salvarosa singing Saule's *Romance of the Willow*, better than Malibran ever could.'

Guy used some appropriate words to express his regret – of which in all truthfulness he only felt an inkling – at having missed the society woman's tune and the virtuoso's gallop. He was a little embarrassed to be amongst these very finely dressed people, with two strips of black silk around his neck instead of two strips of white chiffon and so he sought to make his escape to some corner that was less flooded with light. His involuntary solecism of the dress code would then be more easily concealed by the relative darkness. He had a great deal of difficulty putting this resolution into effect, for Madame d'Ymbercourt kept leading him back to the centre of the circle with a glance, or by saying something requiring an answer, which Guy kept as brief as possible. Finally, however, he managed to reach a doorway leading from the great drawing room to a smaller drawing room: this was laid out as a conservatory, with trellises and fences all covered with camellias.

Madame d'Ymbercourt's drawing room was white and gold and its walls were hung with crimson Indian damask; ample furniture, soft and well-padded, decorated the room. The chandelier with its golden branches had candles that glowed amongst leaves of quartz. Lamps, goblets and a great clock, a testimony to Barbedienne's taste, adorned the white marble fireplace. A beautiful carpet as thick as turf, lay stretched out beneath one's feet. The curtains hung down in front of broad sumptuous windows and in a magnificently framed panel, there was a portrait that smiled even more than the model, a portrait of the countess, painted by Winterhalter.

There was nothing worth saying about this drawing room. It was furnished with beautiful, expensive things but they were things which could be procured by anyone whose financial means allowed them not to dread a lengthy bill from both architect and upholsterer. Its banal richness was perfectly pleasant but it lacked character. Not one feature revealed any choice and if the mistress of the house had been absent one might have thought oneself in the drawing room of a banker or a lawyer or an American in town on a brief visit. Soul and personality were lacking. So, being a natural artist, Guy found this luxury terribly bourgeois and extremely unpleasant. It was, however, the perfect backcloth for Madame d'Ymbercourt, since her beauty was only composed of vulgar perfections.

In the middle of the room was a circular pouffe, on which a great Chinese vase was placed. In it there blossomed a rare exotic plant whose name Madame d'Ymbercourt did not even know and which had been put there by her gardener. Women lounged over the pouffe in dresses of chiffon, and tulle, and lace, and satin, and velvet, with bubbling cascades of fabric that came up to their shoulders; most of them were young and beautiful, their capricious and extravagant outfits a testimony to the endless wealth of Worth's imagination. Their hair was so brown, so blond, so red or powdered that even someone with no malicious intent would have thought art must be embellishing their beauty; quite contrary to the sentiment of Planard's romance. Their hair was piled high with everything that can adorn the head of a fashionable woman: diamonds sparkled, feathers stood erect, leaves scattered with water droplets shone green, real or imitation flowers half opened, little sequin brooches rustled, strings of pearls intertwined, arrows, daggers and two-headed pins gleamed, beetle wing ornamentation shimmered, golden strips of cloth twisted, ribbons of red velvet criss-crossed, star-shapes of precious stones twinkled at the end of their hairsprings, not to mention the grapes and brightly coloured berries which Pomona might lend Flora to add the finishing touch to an evening hairstyle... if a man of letters writing in this year of our Lord 1865 may be allowed to make use of these mythological names.

With his back against the door-frame, Guy gazed upon those satin shoulders covered with their bloom of powder, the backs of their necks with their twists of downy hair, and

43

those white bosoms occasionally betrayed by the shoulder strap of a bodice that was too low – a woman who is sure of her charms easily resigns herself to such little misfortunes. Besides, the movement required to pull the sleeve back into position is one of the most graceful. And a finger correcting the neckline of a dress, to give it a more favourable curve, provides the opportunity for some pretty poses. Our hero indulged in this interesting study, preferring it to banal conversation; in his opinion this was the clearest profit to be drawn from a party or a ball. His eyes flicked through these living volumes of beauty, these animated keepsakes, which society plants in its drawing rooms just as it puts stereoscopes and albums and newspapers on tables for the use of shy people who are embarrassed by their bearing. He felt even safer sampling this pleasure because, following the widespread talk of his coming marriage to Madame d'Ymbercourt, he no longer had to keep a check on his glances. Up until now they had been scrutinised by mothers keen to find a home for their daughters. Nothing more was expected of him now. He had ceased to be a prey. He was a marked man and though more than one woman thought deep down that he might have made a better choice, the thing was accepted. He might even have addressed two or three remarks at a time to a young person without any repercussions. After all, was he not already Madame d'Ymbercourt's husband?

Standing in the same doorway as Monsieur Guy de Malivert was a young man whom he often met at his club and whose cast of mind he quite liked, tinged as it was with an unusual Northern edge. He was the baron de Féroë, a Swedish gentleman and a compatriot of Swedenborg who like him was leaning over the abyss of mysticism, and was, to say the least, as interested in the other world as he was in this one. His head was strange in character. His fair hair, which hung down in almost straight wisps, seemed to be even lighter in colour than his skin and his golden moustache was so pale that one would have thought it was silver. There was an indefinable expression in his blue-grey eyes and their gaze, ordinarily half-veiled by his long whitish lashes, sometimes shot out a piercing flame and seemed to see beyond the scope of humanity. This apart, the baron de Féroë was too perfect a gentleman to affect the slightest eccentricity. His manners were plain and cold, with an English correctness, and in front of a mirror he did not put on the airs of a visionary. That evening, on leaving Madame d'Ymbercourt's tea party, he had to go to a ball at the Austrian Embassy and was therefore in full evening dress: on his black coat, the lapel of which half hid a foreign medal of honour, there shone, hanging on a fine golden chain, the Croix de l'Eléphant and the Croix de Danebrog, the Prussian Order of Merit, the order of Saint-Alexandre Newsky and other decorations from the courts of the North, which bore witness to his diplomatic services.

The baron de Féroë really was a remarkable man, but in a way that was not obvious at first because he wrapped up his character so much in diplomatic composure. He was often to be seen in society, at official receptions, at the club or at the Opéra. But behind this facade of the fashionable man, he lived a mysterious life. He had no intimate friends or companions. In his perfectly kept house, no visitor had ever gone beyond the outer drawing room and the door leading to the other rooms had not been opened for anyone. Like the Turks, he only gave over one room to contact with the outside world and he clearly did not live in this room. Once the visitor had left, he would return to the depths of his apartment. What he busied himself with in there no one knew. Sometimes he would retire there for fairly long periods. Those who noticed his absence attributed it to some secret mission or some trip to Sweden where his family lived. Though if anyone had passed late at night along the little-used street in which the baron lived, they could have seen a light burning at his window; occasionally they might have come across the man himself, leaning his elbows on the balcony, his gaze lost in the stars. But no one had any interest in spying on the baron de Féroë. He gave to society precisely what he owed it and society asks no more than that. With women, his perfect politeness did not exceed certain limits, even when it might have ventured a little further without risking anything. Despite his coldness he was not unpopular. The classic purity of his features recalled Thorwaldsen's greco-scandinavian sculpture. 'He is a frozen Apollo,' the beautiful duchess de C... used to say; and if gossip is to be believed, she had tried to melt that ice.

Like Malivert, the baron de Féroë was looking at a charming snow-white back, slightly arched so that the lines were delightfully rounded. Occasionally it was made to shiver by the imperceptible tickle of a spray of sea-green foliage which had come loose from her hair.

'What a charming creature,' said the baron de Féroë to Guy, whose gaze he had followed. 'Such a shame that she has no soul. Whoever fell in love with her would encounter the same fate as Nathaniel, the student in Hoffmann's *The Sandman*; he would run the risk of clutching a mannequin in his arms at the ball and that is a *danse macabre* for any noble-hearted man.'

'Have no fear, my dear baron,' replied Guy de Malivert, laughing. 'I have no desire to fall in love with the owner of those beautiful shoulders, although in themselves beautiful shoulders are not an object for disdain. At the moment, I shamefully admit it, I don't even feel the ghost of a passion for anyone at all.'

'What?' replied the baron de Féroë with an air of ironic disbelief. 'Not even for Madame d'Ymbercourt, whom you are going to marry, so they say?'

'There are those in the world,' said Malivert, using one of Molière's phrases, 'who would marry the sultan of Turkey and the republic of Venice; I, however, sincerely hope to remain a bachelor.'

'A good idea,' the baron went on and his voice suddenly changed in tone, passing from friendly familiarity to mysterious solemnity. 'Do not engage in any earthly liaison. Keep yourself free for love; it might pay you a visit. The spirits have got their eye on you and in the sphere of the extraterrestrial you might always regret a mistake you made in this world.'

As the young Swedish baron made this strange remark, his steel-blue eyes shone peculiarly and projected rays at the chest of Guy de Malivert, who thought he could feel their heat.

After the strange events of the evening he did not find this mysterious piece of advice as incredible as he would have done the day before. He turned towards his Swedish friend, his eyes astonished and questioning, as though begging the other man to speak more clearly. But Monsieur de Féroë looked at his watch to check the time; said 'I will be very late getting to the Embassy'; shook hands with Malivert quickly and energetically; and without ruffling a dress, stepping on a coat tail or disturbing a flounce, he cut a path towards the door just wide enough for him to pass, with a refined skill that proved how familiar he was with society.

'Well, Guy, won't you come and have a cup of tea?' said Madame d'Ymbercourt, who had finally discovered her supposed admirer, leaning dreamily against the door of the small drawing room. Malivert simply had to follow the mistress of the house to the table where the hot drink was steaming in a silver urn surrounded by cups from China.

Reality was trying to regain its hold over idealism.

CHAPTER 3

The baron de Féroë's strange remark, and the almost immediate disappearance of the young diplomat after making it, set Guy's imagination working while he was returning to the district of Saint-Germain carried swiftly along by Grymalkin's rapid trot. An icy North wind made it pleasant for the horse to think of returning to the stable, to its nice warm box fitted out with a bed of straw, although being the well-bred animal that it was, it would not have needed this motivation to keep up a quick pace.

'What the devil could he have meant by those grave riddles of his,' thought Guy de Malivert. 'Spouting them out in that tone of voice, he sounded like an occult priest.' He dropped his clothing into Jack's hands. 'And yet the baron de Féroë comes from the most unromantic of civilisations; he is precise and polite and as sharp as an English razor; his manners are exquisite but so cold as to make the Arctic wind seem warm. It is inconceivable that he should have wanted to play a trick on me. No one makes fun of Guy de Malivert, not even the courageous Swede with the white eyelashes; anyway, what would be funny about a joke like that? He derived no pleasure from it in any case, for he shied away immediately, like a man who wants to say no more on the subject. Oh, I must stop dreaming up such nonsense. I'll see the baron tomorrow at the club and I'm sure he'll be more forthcoming. I'll get off to bed now and try to get some sleep, whether the spirits are watching me or not.'

Guy did go to bed but sleep did not come to him as he had hoped, even though he called to his aid the most soporific pamphlets and read them with an extremely intense mechanical concentration. Despite himself, he listened out for the imperceptible sounds which still issue from even the most perfect silence. The catch of the alarm mechanism on his clock before it chimed the hour or the half-hour; a crackling of sparks amongst the ashes; the snap of the panelling that had contracted with the heat; the sound of a drop of oil dripping in his lamp; the puff of air being drawn into the fireplace and whistling low under the door despite the draught excluders; the unexpected fall of a newspaper from his bed on to the floor. His nerves were so on edge that all these things made him tremble, as he might have done if a firearm had suddenly gone off. His hearing was now so acute that he could hear his arteries pulsating and his heartbeat ringing out in his throat. But amid all these confused murmurings, he could perceive nothing resembling a sigh.

He closed his eyes from time to time in the hope that drowsiness would follow, but before long he reopened them and scrutinised the nooks and crannies of the room with a sense of curiosity that was not without apprehension. Guy really longed to see something and yet he dreaded his wish being granted. Occasionally his dilated pupils imagined they made out vague forms in the corners which were not reached by the light from the lamp with the green shade. The folds of the curtains took on the appearance of feminine clothing and seemed to twitch as though stirred by the movement of a body. But this was a pure illusion. Flashes and spots of light, changing patterned patches, butterflies and wavy worm-like pieces of string all danced and swarmed, growing larger, then shrinking before his tired eyes, with which he could discern virtually nothing.

He was more perturbed than words can say and, despite seeing and hearing nothing, he could sense the presence of the unknown spirit in his room. He got up, slipped on a camel hair mach'lah which he had brought back from Cairo, threw two or three logs on to the embers and sat down near the hearth in a big armchair. This is more comfortable for the insomniac than a bed which has been rumpled by a fevered, sleepless night. On the carpet near the chair he saw a crumpled piece of paper and picked it up. It was the letter he had been writing to Madame d'Ymbercourt under that strange impulse which he could not yet fathom. He picked it up, smoothed out the folds and on examining it with care he noticed that the style of the handwriting did not look quite like his own. It was as though these lines had been penned by an impatient hand which, in its attempts to create a duplicate, was incapable of forcing itself to copy the original exactly; as though it had mixed in with the letters of the original the upstrokes and downstrokes of its own handwriting. Its appearance was more elegant, more slender and more feminine.

As he noticed these details, Guy de Malivert was musing on the *Gold Bug* by Edgar Allan Poe and on the marvellous shrewdness with which William Legrand managed to discover the meaning of the coded letter in which Captain Kidd enigmatically names the exact location of the hiding place which conceals his treasures. Guy would very much like to have possessed this profound sense of intuition which produces such daring and accurate assumptions, filling in the gaps and then repairing the web of broken connections. In this instance, however, Legrand himself could have joined forces with Auguste Dupin from *The Purloined Letter* and *The Murders in the Rue Morgue* and still it would have remained humanly impossible for him to have divined the secret force which had caused Malivert's hand to lose control.

Eventually, though, Guy fell into a heavy, awkward sleep, the kind that follows a sleepless night and is brought on by the approach of sunrise. He woke when Jack came in to relight the fire and to help his master get washed and dressed. Guy was feeling shivery and uncomfortable; he yawned, stretched, shook himself and splashed cold water over his face. Revived by these bracing ablutions, he was soon himself again. The grey-eyed morn, as Shakespeare said, came down not over the green hillsides but over the white rooftops; it slid into the apartment, whose curtains and shutters Jack had opened, and gave each thing its real appearance once more, chasing away the imaginings of the night. Nothing is as reassuring as sunlight, even when it is just a pale winter's sun. It was this kind of sun which now penetrated the leaves of the trees, leaves which had already left a silvery glaze of frost on the windowpanes.

Now that Malivert was again experiencing the normal feelings of life, he was shocked by the disturbed night he had had. 'I never knew I had such a nervous disposition,' he said to himself. And he tore the wrappers from around the newspapers which had just been brought up to him. He glanced at the serialised story sections, read the miscellaneous news articles, took up the copy of *Evangeline* which he had put down the day before, and smoked a cigar. These various activities took him to eleven o' clock, at which time he dressed and to get a little exercise he set himself the task of walking to the café Bignon for lunch. A morning frost had hardened the night's snow and as he passed through the Tuileries gardens Malivert enjoyed seeing the mythological statues sprinkled with white powder and the great chestnut trees all covered with a silvery fur. He ate a good, light lunch, like a man who wants to make up for a tiring previous day. He chatted animatedly with merry companions, who were the finest wits and sceptics in Paris and had adopted the Greek maxim 'Remember to disbelieve' as their motto. But when the jokes went too far, Guy's smile seemed a little forced. He did not abandon himself wholeheartedly to the incredulous paradoxes or to the cynical bragging. The baron de Féroë's remark, 'The spirits have got their eye on you', kept coming into his head involuntarily and he felt that there was something mysterious watching him from behind. He stood up and shook the hands of those with whom he had been chatting. Then he walked up and down the boulevard: more spiritual activity goes on there in one day than in a year throughout the whole of the rest of the globe. Finding it somewhat deserted because of the time and the cold, and without thinking, he mechanically turned the corner of Rue de la Chaussée-d'Antin. Soon he was in front of Madame d'Ymbercourt's house. As he was about to ring the doorbell, he thought he felt something blowing in his ear; and in this breath he thought he heard these words whispered very quietly and yet distinctly: 'Do not go in.' He turned around briskly and saw no one.

'Oh, honestly!' said Malivert to himself. 'Am I going mad?

Am I hallucinating in broad daylight now? Should I obey this bizarre command or not?'

The sudden movement he had made in order to turn around had caused his hand to let go of the bell-pull on which it had been placed. The spring had been activated and had made the bell vibrate. The door had opened and the doorman now stood in front of his lodge, looking at Malivert as he hesitated on the doorstep. Malivert went in though he had not the slightest desire to do so, following the supernatural incident that had just occurred. He was received by Madame d'Ymbercourt in the small drawing room, where she took morning visits. It was decorated in buttercup yellow, embellished with blue. Guy found the shade particularly unpleasant. 'Yellow is the best colour to set off a brunette, is it not?' was the countess's reply to Malivert, who had on more than one occasion dared to request that this odious wall covering be changed.

Madame d'Ymbercourt was dressed in a black taffeta skirt and a garish embroidered jacket, laden with more jet and braid than any *maja* going to a *feria* or bullfight ever hung from her basque costume. Although the countess was a society woman, she made the mistake of letting herself be dressed in the kind of ridiculous costumes that are only worn by the kind of dolls with pink cheeks and simpering expressions that are depicted in fashion plates.

Somewhat unusually, Madame d'Ymbercourt was looking serious; a cloud of annoyance darkened her normally serene forehead and the corners of her mouth sloped downwards. One of her good friends had just left her, having asked her with the feigned bonhomie that women show on such occasions, what was the date that had been fixed for her marriage to Guy de Malivert. The countess had blushed, stammered and replied vaguely that it would happen soon. Society had given her Guy as a husband, though he had never asked for her hand or made any formal declaration. Madame d'Ymbercourt put this down to a respectful shyness and also perhaps to the feeling of uncertainty every young man experiences when he abandons his bachelor's life of liberty. But she firmly believed he would propose some day or other. And she so much regarded herself to be his wife that she had already worked out in her head the special arrangements which the presence of a husband in the house would require. 'This is Guy's bedroom; this is his study; and this is his smoking room,' she had said to herself more than once as she sized up certain rooms within her suites.

Though she was scarcely to his taste, Guy had to admit that Madame d'Ymbercourt was beautiful in the conventional sense; she also retained an unblemished reputation and possessed a quite considerable fortune. But he was far from spellbound and, like anyone whose heart is empty, he had allowed himself to get used to this house where he was given a better welcome than in any other. He had returned because after a few days' absence an amiable but insistent note forced him to reappear.

Why, in any case, would he not have gone? Madame d'Ymbercourt received quite good company and on certain days he would meet some of his friends there. It would have been less convenient for him to seek them out amongst the scattered population of Paris.

'You're looking rather unwell,' said Malivert to the countess. 'Might it be that your night was disturbed by the little devils in your green tea?'

'Oh no. I put so much cream in it that it loses all its strength. Besides I'm the Mithridates of tea: it no longer affects me. No, it's not that, I'm just annoyed.'

'Have I timed my visit badly? Am I disturbing some of your plans? If so, I will leave and it will be as though I hadn't found you at home and had just left my card with your doorman.'

'You're not disturbing me at all and you know that I'm always pleased to see you,' replied the countess. 'Perhaps I shouldn't say this but your visits actually seem to me to be quite rare, though to others they might seem too frequent.'

'You're a free agent, are you not? You have no tiresome relatives, no troublesome brother, no drivelling uncle, no chaperone aunt sitting in the window doing her tapestry work.

53

Your obliging nature has rid you of the mass of unpleasant individuals that all too often spring up around a pretty woman, and left you with just their legacy. You can receive whomever you like, because you are dependent on no one.'

'That is true,' replied Madame d'Ymbercourt. 'I'm not dependent on anyone. And yet I'm dependent on everyone. A woman is never emancipated, even if she is a widow and apparently mistress of her actions. A whole police force of disinterested guardians surrounds her and attends to her affairs. And so, Guy, you're compromising my reputation.'

'Me, compromising your reputation!' exclaimed Malivert, with a surprised sincerity that testified to a sense of modesty very rare in a young man of 28, who is well turned out in trousers imported from England and clothes from Renard. 'Why me rather than d'Aversac, Beaumont, Yanowski or Féroë, who are here extremely regularly?'

'I couldn't say,' replied the countess. 'Perhaps you're unwittingly dangerous or perhaps society has recognised a force in you of which you yourself are unaware. None of those gentlemen's names has been brought up. It is thought quite natural they should come to my Wednesday soirées, pay me a few visits between five and six o' clock on their way back from a lakeside walk, and greet me in my box at the Opéra or at the Bouffons. These actions are innocent in themselves but when it is you that does them, they become terribly important, it seems.'

'But I'm the plainest fellow in the world. No one has ever said anything about me. I haven't got a blue tailcoat like Werther and I haven't got a doublet with slashes like Don Juan. You don't ever see me playing the guitar beneath a balcony. And I don't go to the races in a shooting-brake with ostentatiously dressed little ladies. At parties I don't debate any sentimental questions with pretty women to bring a glow to the pure delicacy of my heart. You don't see me standing against a column with my hand in my waistcoat looking sombre and fatal as I look silently at a pale and beautiful woman with long ringlets like Alfred de Vigny's Kitty Bell. Do I have twists of hair around my fingers and a sachet of violets she's given me held to my breast? Search my most intimate drawers and you'll find no portraits of blondes or brunettes, no bundles of perfumed letters tied with a ribbon or a rubber fastener, no embroidered slippers, no lace-edged masks, nor any of the trinkets that lovers use to create their own private museums. Do I honestly look like a lucky man?'

'You are very modest,' Madame d'Ymbercourt went on. 'Or else you delight in making yourself out to be innocent. Unfortunately, however, not everyone shares your view. There are those who find fault with the attention you pay me, though I myself see nothing wrong with it.'

'Then I shall space out my visits,' said Malivert. 'I shall only come once a fortnight or once a month; and then I shall travel. Where shall I go? Let me see: I know Spain, Italy, Germany and Russia quite well; what if I were to go to Greece? It's criminal never to have seen Athens, the Acropolis and the Parthenon. You can go via Marseilles or set off from Trieste on an Austrian Lloyds' steamer. You call at Corfu, you see Ithaca as you pass by – *soli occidenti bene objacentem* – basking in today's setting sun as it did in Homer's time. You go down to the heel of the Gulf of Lepanto. You cross the Isthmus and you see the remains of Corinth, where not everyone was allowed to go. Another boat picks you up and in a few hours, you're at Piraeus. Beaumont told me all that. He left here the ardent romantic. Over there he got his metope on the brain and now he wants nothing to do with cathedrals. He's become the rigid classicist. He claims that since the time of the Greeks humanity has regressed to a state of barbarism and that our supposed civilisations are only various forms of decadence.'

Madame d'Ymbercourt was not particularly flattered by this geographical lyricism. She saw in Guy de Malivert a readiness not to compromise her that was a little too keen. To take his concern for her reputation as far as to run away, did not gratify her.

'Who wants you to go to Greece?' she said to Guy. 'Besides,' she added, blushing slightly, her voice trembling

55

imperceptibly, 'wouldn't there be a far simpler way to silence the scandalmongering, a way that would avoid leaving your friends and risking your neck in a country which is scarcely safe, if one is to believe *The King of the Mountains* by Edmond About?'

Afraid that she might have made too blatant a remark, the countess felt a cloud of pink, more marked than the first, cover her face and neck. Her breathing had quickened a little, making the golden-threaded jet on her jacket shine and rustle on her bosom. Taking courage once more, she raised her eyes towards Malivert. A glow of emotion made them truly beautiful. Madame d'Ymbercourt loved Guy, her all too silent admirer, as much as any woman of her kind *can* love. The casual yet neat way he wore his tie pleased her; and with that profound feminine logic, whose deductions the most perceptive philosophers have trouble following, she had inferred from the knot of this tie that Malivert possessed all the necessary characteristics to make an excellent husband. The only problem was that this husband-to-be was walking extremely slowly towards the altar and seemed in no great hurry to light the torches for the marriage.

Guy understood exactly what Madame d'Ymbercourt meant; but more than ever he dreaded committing himself with an unwise remark. He responded: 'No doubt, no doubt, but taking a trip calls a halt to everything and when you get back you can see the best thing to do.'

Hearing such a vague and cold reply, the countess flinched and bit her lip. Guy was extremely embarrassed and kept quiet. The situation was becoming increasingly strained when the valet came and created a useful diversion by announcing: the baron de Féroë.

CHAPTER 4

Seeing the Swedish baron come in, Malivert could not help
uttering a slight sigh of satisfaction. He looked up at Monsieur de Féroë with gratitude written all over his face, for no
visit had ever been better timed. Had it not been for this
opportune interruption, Guy would have found himself in a
remarkably embarrassing situation; he would have had to
give Madame d'Ymbercourt a categorical reply and he hated
nothing more than these brutally formal explanations. He
preferred to keep a promise than make one, and even over
matters to which he was indifferent he took care not to
commit himself one way or another. The glance Madame
d'Ymbercourt shot at the baron de Féroë was not marked
with the same benevolence as the one he had got from Malivert. And if it were not accepted practice in society to learn
how to dissimulate one's feelings, one would have been able
to read a mixture of reproach, impatience and anger in this
brief glance. The appearance of this unfortunate character
had blown away an opportunity which perhaps would not
recur for a long time and which it had cost Madame
d'Ymbercourt dear to engineer: Guy certainly would not
seek out another opportunity and would even take care to
avoid one. Although in clearly defined cases Guy would have
shown decisiveness and courage, he was somewhat apprehen-
sive about something which might tie him down in some
way or other. His intelligence gave him access to every career
but he had not wanted to pursue any: the route he chose
might have diverted him from the right path. He had no
known ties, except the unappealing habit which drew him
back to the countess's home more often than anywhere else;
it was this that made people think they planned to marry.
Every kind of bond or obligation inspired disdain in him and
one would have thought that, motivated by a secret instinct,
he was trying to conserve his freedom for some later event.

After exchanging the initial formalities, the vague pleasant-ries which serve as the prelude to conversation, in the way one tests out a keyboard before tackling the piece of music, the baron de Féroë made one of those transitions that within two sentences takes one from the fall of Nineveh to the triumphant success of *Le Gladiateur*, and put forward an aes-thetic and transcendental thesis on Wagner's more abstruse operas, *The Flying Dutchman*, *Lohengrin* and *Tristan and Isolde*. Although Madame d'Ymbercourt was quite an able pianist and one of Herz's most accomplished students, she under-stood nothing about music. This was especially true of such profound, mysterious and complicated music as that of the maestro, the man whose *Tannhäuser* aroused such a violent storm in France. She responded from time to time to the baron's enthusiastic analyses, all the while adding a few stitches to a strip of tapestry she had taken from a basket placed near the armchair where she normally sat, not far from the fireplace; her objections were banal and the kind which are often made about all kinds of new music. It was directed just as much at Rossini as it now is at Wagner: the music lacks rhythm, it is devoid of melody, it is obscure, it overdoes the brass, the orchestration is inextricably compli-cated, it is a deafening racket and finally it is a physical impossibility to perform it.

'Now, that is what I consider to be a most learned disserta-tion, though when it comes to music, I'm an awful ignora-mus; I am moved by whatever I find attractive. I admire Beethoven and even Verdi, although that might not be read-ily accepted now that one has to be for the queen's corner or for the king's, as it was in the time of the rivalry between the supporters of Gluck and Piccini. I will leave the rest of you to fight it out, as I am unable to shed any light on the discussion; at best I could utter the odd 'hem, hem!', like the Minim who was made the arbiter in a philosophical discus-sion between Molière and Chapelle.'

Having said these words, Guy de Malivert rose to take his leave. Madame d'Ymbercourt, whose hand he shook in the English manner, fixed her gaze on him, which meant 'Stay' as obviously as a society woman's reserve allows. This gaze followed Malivert obliquely as far as the door; it was tinged with a sadness which would no doubt have touched him had he been able to perceive it. But his attention was taken up by the Swede's imperiously tranquil face, which seemed to say: 'Do not expose yourself again to the peril from which I have saved you.'

When he was in the street, he thought, not without a certain fear, about the supernatural warning he had received before going into Madame d'Ymbercourt's house and about the baron de Féroë's visit which coincided so strangely with the way he had disobeyed that mysterious piece of advice. The baron seemed to have been sent to support him by occult forces, whose presence he felt vaguely about him. Without being a committed disbeliever and sceptic, Guy de Malivert was not someone to whom faith came easily and he had never been seen lapsing into the reveries brought about by hypnotists, séance tables and spirit-rappers. He even felt a kind of revulsion for those experiences to which people want to add regular doses of the supernatural and he had refused to see the famous Home, who at one time captivated the whole of Paris. Just the day before, he had been living the life of a care-free bachelor; he had been in good humour and on the whole quite happy to be in the world; he didn't cut too bad a figure and he was enclosed in the circle of visible things, not caring whether or not the planet carried with it, on its revolutions around the sun, an atmosphere enlivened by a population of invisible and intangible beings. Yet he had to admit that the conditions of his life had changed; a new element, though he could not have put a name to it, was seeking to introduce itself into his existence, which until then had been so peaceful and from which he had been careful to banish anything likely to cause trouble. As yet, he had very little evidence: a feeble sigh like a groan from an aeolian harp, a substitution of thought in a mechanically written letter, three words whispered in his ear, and the encounter with a fateful and solemn-looking Swedish baron; but it was clear that the spirit was circling around him *quoerens quem devoret*, as the Bible says in its eternal wisdom.

While he mused in this vein, Guy de Malivert had arrived at the roundabout on the Champs-Elysées, though he had no more cause to go in that direction than in any other. His body had carried him this way and he had gone along with it. There were not many people about: the odd few stubborn characters, who exercise for health reasons regardless of the season and make holes in the ice on the rivers so they can bathe, were coming back from the Bois de Boulogne with blue noses and purple cheeks, riding horses protected with kneepads. Two or three of them gave Guy a friendly wave. Though he was on foot, he even got a gracious smile from one of the famous characters of the *demi-monde*, who was displaying in an open carriage the splendid range of furs she had acquired in Russia.

'It's because I'm the only member of the public about, that people are vying for my approbation,' thought Malivert. 'Cora wouldn't have greeted me like that in summer. What the devil have I come here for, anyway? It's not the time of year to dine in an arbour or at the Moulin Rouge or with Marco or the baroness d'Ange. Besides I'm in no mood for having fun. As Rabelais said, when the moustache begins to show again, it is time to dream. And there behind the Arc de l'Etoile you can see the setting sun.'

Indeed the arch of this huge gateway opening out on to the sky, framed a picture of a strange bank of clouds with a silhouetted outline that was bordered with a lather of light. The evening wind made these floating shapes tremble slightly, giving them a kind of life of their own. It was like those illustrations by Gustave Doré, where the reveries that haunt the character's mind are reflected in the clouds: the Wandering Jew is shown Christ climbing the Mount of Calvary and Don Quixote is shown wandering knights in battle with sorcerers. Likewise one could easily have found figures and groups of people in this dark hazy mass shot through with beams of light. Malivert thought he could make out angels with great wings of fire soaring over a swarm of indistinct creatures that writhed on a bank of black clouds like a promontory bathed in shadow amid a phosphorescent sea.

Occasionally one of the background figures left the crowd and came up to the illuminated areas crossing the red disc of the sun. Once it had got there, it flew for a moment alongside one of the angels and melted into light. No doubt, a degree of imagination was needed to fill out this jerky, changing sketch. A cloud scene can be described as Hamlet described it to Polonius: 'It is a camel, that is unless it is a whale.' And in both cases it is quite valid to reply in the affirmative, without necessarily being an idiotic sycophant.

As night fell, it extinguished this hazy phantasmagoria. The gas being lit at the top of the streetlamps soon traced two magical strings of light from Place de la Concorde to the Arc de l'Etoile; strangers coming into Paris of an evening are impressed by this triumphal avenue. Guy hailed a cab that was cruising around looking for a fare and got himself taken to Rue de Choiseul, where his club was located. Leaving his jacket in the hands of the uniformed servants who stood in the ante-room, he leafed through the register which logs the names of the people dining that day and was glad to see the name of the baron de Féroë. He wrote his own below, then crossed the billiards room where the referee was waiting in melancholy mood for a couple of these gentlemen to be taken with the whim to come and play a frame. He passed through several other vast, high rooms furnished with all the modern comforts one might desire, and kept at a constant temperature by a powerful heater; which is not to say there were not huge logs burning down to embers on the monumental firedogs of the great fireplaces. There were scarcely four or five of the club's members there, lounging on divans or sitting with their elbows on the big green table in the reading room. Casually they perused the newspapers and reviews – arranged in a methodical order which was constantly being disturbed and re-established. Two or three of them were dispatching love letters and business correspondence on club paper.

Dinner time was approaching and those present were chatting amongst themselves as they waited for the head waiter to announce that dinner was served. Guy was beginning to worry that the baron de Féroë would not come but as everyone was going into the dining room he arrived and took his seat next to Monsieur de Malivert. The dinner was served with great pomp – there was crystal and silverware and silver plate-warmers. It was quite a light meal and everyone washed it down in their own way, one drinking Bordeaux, another drinking champagne, a third drinking pale ale, according to their fancy or habit. Some had quite an anglicised taste and asked for a glass of sherry or port, which was brought to them ceremoniously by tall servants in short trousers on trays decorated with the club's insignia in guilloche. Each man indulged his own whim without worrying about his neighbour because everyone feels at home at the club.

Quite unusually Guy did little justice to his dinner. Half the dishes got left on his plate and the bottle of Château Margaux placed in front of him was emptied only very slowly.

'There would be no cause to reproach you,' said the baron de Féroë, 'as the angel of light once reproached Swedenborg, saying: 'You eat too much'. You're a fine example of abstemiousness this evening; one would think you were trying to spiritualise yourself by fasting.'

'I don't know,' replied Guy 'whether a few mouthfuls more or less would release soul from material being and make more diaphanous the veils which separate invisible things from visible things, but I don't have much of an appetite. Certain circumstances of which you seem to be aware have, I admit, been startling me since yesterday and have made me more preoccupied than I usually am. In my normal state I am not distracted at the dinner table but today other thoughts control me against my will. Have you any plans for this evening, baron? If you have nothing worthwhile or pleasant to do, I'd suggest that after coffee we smoke some cigars together on the divan in the little music room. We won't be disturbed there, as long as none of these gentlemen takes it into his head to attack the piano, and that is most unlikely. Our musicians are all absent this evening: they're busy watching the public rehearsal for the new opera.'

The baron de Féroë went along with Malivert's proposal in the most polite manner and replied graciously that there could be no better way of spending time. As the two gentlemen settled themselves on the divan and concerned themselves first of all with drawing regular puffs from excellent cigars from *la Vuelta de Abajo*, each of them mused on the necessarily bizarre discussion which would soon be underway. After making a few observations on the quality of the tobacco they were smoking and on the preference that must be accorded dark outer leaves over mild ones, the Swedish baron himself brought up the subject which Malivert had been burning to broach.

'First of all I must apologise for having taken the liberty of giving you that enigmatic advice the other evening at Madame d'Ymbercourt's. You hadn't confided in me and it was somewhat indiscreet of me to have entered into your thoughts without your having opened them up to me. It's not my style to swap my role as society man for that of wizard and I wouldn't have done it if I hadn't taken a lively interest in you and recognised signs which are perceptible only to the initiated; these revealed that you had recently received a visit from a spirit or at the very least that the invisible world was endeavouring to communicate with you.'

Guy swore that the baron had not offended him in any way and that in such a novel situation, he was, on the contrary, extremely glad to have encountered a guide who seemed so familiar with supernatural things and whose serious character was perfectly well-known to him.

'You understand,' replied the baron with a slight nod of gratitude, 'that I don't find it easy to abandon this reserve. But perhaps you've seen enough to believe that everything doesn't end where our senses stop. I'm not worried any more if our discussion tends towards these mysterious subjects, or if you take me for a visionary or a crank. My position puts me above any suspicions of charlatanism and besides I only let the world see my superficial life. I won't ask you what has happened to you but I can see that you are of interest to those outside the sphere in which ordinary life is normally enclosed.'

'Yes,' said Guy de Malivert, 'something indefinable is floating around me and I don't think I'm committing an indiscretion towards the spirits, with whom you're on the best of terms, by telling you in detail what you sensed with your superhuman intuition.' And Guy related to the baron de Féroë the events which had made the previous evening quite remarkable.

The Swedish baron listened to him, spinning the end of his pale golden moustache with extreme care, but without showing the slightest surprise. He remained silent for a moment and seemed to be lost in profound reflection; then, as though this remark summoned up a whole chain of inner thoughts, he suddenly said to Guy:

'Monsieur de Malivert, has a girl ever died of love for you?'

'Not a girl nor a young woman, at least as far as I know,' replied Malivert. 'I'm not so fatuous as to think I can inspire such despair. My love affairs, if the careless kisses of two whimsical liaisons may be called by such a name, were very calm, not very romantic and as easily undone as begun. So as to avoid emotional scenes which I abhor, I've always arranged things so that *I* am betrayed and abandoned; my pride being perfectly willing to make this small sacrifice for my peace of mind. So I don't think I've left behind many inconsolable Ariadnes in my life; in those little tales of Parisian mythology, the arrival of Bacchus regularly preceded the departure of Theseus. Besides, at the risk of giving you a poor idea of my capacity for emotion, I must confess that I have never felt for anyone that intense, exclusive, frantic passion that everyone talks about, without perhaps having experienced it. No living thing has inspired in me the notion of attaching myself to it indissolubly; no living thing has made me dream of planning the fusion of two existences into a single one, escaping to an azure paradise of light and coolness which they say love can build even in a hut or an attic.

'That doesn't mean, my dear Guy, that you aren't capable

64

of passion. There are many kinds of love and no doubt when the fate of souls was decided, you were reserved for a higher destiny. But there is still time. Only our consenting desire gives the spirits access to us. You are on the verge of a limitless world, which is profound and mysterious and full of illusions and darkness, and where there is combat between good and bad influences that you must be able to discern. There are marvels to see and there are terrifying things that can disturb human reason. No one returns from the depths of this abyss without bearing an indelible paleness on his face; the eye of the flesh cannot contemplate with impunity what is reserved for the eye of the soul; these trips outside our sphere cause inexpressible weariness and at the same time inspire hopeless nostalgia. Stop on this fearsome brink, don't pass over from one world to the other and don't respond to the call which seeks to entice you out of your sentient life. Those who make these suggestions are safe within the circle they draw around themselves, a circle through which the spirits cannot break. Let reality be your circle; do not leave it, or else your powers will cease. You can see that for a hierophant, I'm not exactly keen on proselytising.'

'So,' said Malivert, 'do I have something to fear from making perilous adventures into this invisible world around us, whose presence is only revealed to a small number of privileged people?'

'No,' replied the baron de Féroë. 'Nothing that is perceptible to the human eye will happen to you. But your soul may remain profoundly and eternally disturbed.'

'So does the spirit that is honouring me with its attention have a dangerous nature?'

'It's a spirit of friendship, benevolence and love. I encountered it in an environment of light but in its own way the sky can make people dizzy just like chasms can. Remember the tale of the shepherd who was in love with a star.'

'But,' replied Malivert, 'the remark you made to me at Madame d'Ymbercourt's seemed to be a warning not to involve myself in any terrestrial relationship.'

'I had to say that,' responded the baron de Féroë. 'You had

to be warned to keep yourself free, in case you should respond to the manifestations of the spirit. But because you haven't yet done so, you'll notice you're still in possession of yourself. Perhaps you'd be better off staying that way and continuing your normal life.'

'And marrying Madame d'Ymbercourt, I suppose,' replied Guy de Malivert with an ironic smile.

'Why not?' said the baron de Féroë. 'She's young, she's beautiful, she loves you and I've seen real distress in her eyes at your oblique refusal. It wouldn't be impossible for her to acquire a soul.'

'That is a risk I don't want to run. I understand your concern, dear baron, but don't strive so hard to tie me back down to a vulgar existence. I am freer of it than one might initially think. I might have organised my material life in a pleasant and comfortable way but that doesn't prove any sensuality on my part. Material well-being is basically of complete indifference to me. I may have found it more convenient to appear carefree and merry than to affect tasteless fits of romantic depression but it does not follow that I am contented or charmed by the world as it is. It is true that in a drawing room, with a circle of pretentious women around me, I don't talk about affairs of the heart or passion or the ideal. But I have kept my soul proud and pure and free of any vulgar cult as I wait for the god unknown.'

As Malivert talked like this, with more fire than society people put into what they say, the baron de Féroë's eyes sparkled and his face took on an expression of enthusiasm which was ordinarily hidden beneath a mask of icy indifference.

He was glad to see that Guy was resisting prosaic temptation and maintaining his spiritual will.

'You've made your decision, my dear Guy, so go home; you're sure to receive further communication. I shall stay here; I won 100 louis from d'Aversac yesterday; I owe him a chance to get his revenge.

'The opera rehearsal must be over: I can hear our friends

coming back, humming themes they can't remember in their utterly tuneless voices.

'Make your escape; this hullabaloo will put your soul out of key.'

Guy shook the baron's hand and got into his carriage, which was waiting for him at the door of the club.

CHAPTER 5

Guy de Malivert returned home absolutely resolute that he would embark on the adventure. He might not have appeared romantic, but he was nonetheless; a lofty and timid sense of propriety, however, made him hide his feelings, and he asked no more of the world than he gave to it. Pleasantly indifferent relationships linked him to society without chaining him down, and they were links which it was always easy to cast off. Understandably though, his soul was imagining a happiness that he had never yet encountered.

Following the baron de Féroë's remarks to him at the club about the need to project the desire to call up the spirits from the depths of the invisible world to the bounds of this one, Malivert summoned all the powers of his being and formulated within himself the desire to enter into more direct communication with the mysterious spirit which he sensed was around him and which could not really object to being evoked because it had tried to manifest itself of its own accord.

Having done that, Malivert, who was in his studio-cum-drawing room where he was at the start of this tale, began to look and listen with extreme concentration. He saw and heard nothing at first and yet the objects which furnished the room – statuettes, pictures, old sculpted sideboards, exotic curiosities and shooting trophies – seemed to him to have taken on a strange appearance which they did not normally have. The lights and the shadows cast by the lamp lent them a fantastic life of their own. A jade magot seemed to be laughing from ear to ear in a way that was childlike and old at the same time, and a Venus de Milo, whose pointed breasts were illuminated by a ray of light against a dark background, flared her proud nostrils in pique and scornfully lowered the corners of her arc-shaped mouth. The Chinese god and the Greek goddess disapproved of Malivert's venture. At least that is what one might have believed by the expressions they assumed in this light. Imperceptibly Malivert's eyes, as though prompted by a warning from within, turned their attention towards a Venetian mirror which hung from the leather tapestry from Cordoba.

It was one of those mirrors from the last century, the kind one often sees in scenes by Longhi, the Watteau of Venetian decadence, that show people getting dressed up and setting off for a ball. One still comes across a few of them on bric-a-brac stalls in the Ghetto. The bevel-edged mirror was framed with cut crystal ornamentation and topped with a jumble of foliage and flowers in the same material which, against the uniform colouring of the background, sometimes took on the appearance of unpolished silver, and sometimes through its facets shot out prismatic flashes. At the centre of this glistening surround, the mirror, whose dimensions were small like all Venetian mirrors, seemed to be a blueish black, indefinably profound, and like an opening made on to a void full of perfect darkness.

Strangely, none of the objects opposite it were reflected in it: it was just like one of those theatrical mirrors which the scene-painter covers with vague neutral colours to stop it reflecting the auditorium.

A vague instinct gave Malivert the premonition that if something were to be revealed to him that night, it would be through this medium. He never usually set his eyes on the mirror but now it was exerting a kind of fascination over him and absorbing his gaze in an overwhelming way. But however fixedly he locked his gaze on that point, he could distinguish nothing but a blackness made even more mysteriously intense by the strips of crystal. Finally he thought that within this darkness he could make out a kind of vague milky whiteness, a kind of distant flickering glow which seemed to be getting nearer. He turned round to see what object in the room could be projecting this reflection; he saw nothing. Though Malivert was brave and had proved it on many an occasion, he could not stop himself feeling the hair bristle on his skin, and the little shiver that Job mentions running over his flesh. This time he was going to cross that fearsome threshold of his own free will, and in full knowledge of what was happening. He was placing his foot outside the circle which nature has traced around man. His life could be thrown out of orbit to revolve for ever about an unknown point. Though disbelievers might laugh, no course of action was ever taken with more seriousness and Guy sensed the full importance of it; but an irresistible attraction was dragging him along and he continued obstinately to plunge his eyes deep into the Venetian mirror. What would he see? In what guise would the spirit present itself so as to be perceptible by a human being. Would it be a graceful figure or a terrible figure? Would it bring joy or terror? Although the glow in the mirror had not yet taken on any distinct form, Guy was convinced it would prove to be a feminine spirit. The sigh he had heard the day before resonated too tenderly in his heart for it not to be.

Had it belonged to this earth or did it come from a higher domain or a distant planet? That was something he could not know. However, remembering the baron de Féroë's question, he thought it must be a soul which had been through the conditions of terrestrial life and which was being attracted back to its former sphere. No doubt he would discover its motive at a later stage.

The patch of light in the mirror was beginning to form a more distinct image and paint itself in a wash of pale colours which were somehow ethereal and which would have made the tones of the brightest palette look dull. It was more the notion of a colour than the colour itself, a haze shot through with light and so delicately nuanced that all the words known to man could not describe it. Guy kept on looking, the victim of an emotional state of nervous anxiety. The image became increasingly condensed though without attaining the vulgar precision of reality. And Guy de Malivert was at last able to see, defined by the border of the mirror like a portrait in its frame, the head of a young woman; or rather a girl. Mortal beauty is only the shadow of such beauty. A pinkish paleness faintly coloured this head where light and

70

shade were hardly perceptible. Unlike terrestrial faces its form did not need this contrast since it was not subjected to the light that shines on us. Her hair was the colour of a halo. It softened the line of her forehead like a golden vapour. In her half-lowered eyes swam infinitely gentle, night-blue irises which brought to mind the parts of the sky that are invaded at sunset by the violet shades of evening. Her nose was fine and thin and quite delicate. A smile in the Leonardo da Vinci style, but with greater tenderness and less irony, gave her lips an adorable curve. Her supple neck was bowed forward slightly as though under the weight of her head; it disappeared into a silvery half-light which would have lit up any other face.

This feeble sketch, necessarily done in words that were created to describe the things of our world, can only give a very vague idea of the apparition Guy de Malivert was contemplating in the Venetian mirror. Was he seeing it with the eye of his flesh or with the eye of his soul? Did the image exist in reality and could someone, who had not been filled with the same nervous impulse as Guy, have perceived it? This is not an easy question to answer; but whatever the case, what he was seeing, though it was *similar*, did not *resemble* in any way what passes in this life for the head of a beautiful woman. They were, it is true, the same features, but purified, transfigured, idealised and rendered perceptible by a somehow immaterial substance, which barely had the necessary density to be made out in the earth's crass atmosphere by eyes whose veils have still not fallen away. The spirit or soul which was communicating with Guy de Malivert had clearly taken on the form of its old perishable shell, but it looked the way it would have in a more subtle, ethereal environment where only the phantoms of things, and not the things themselves, can live. This vision plunged Guy into ineffable raptures. The feeling of fear he had experienced at first had subsided and he succumbed unreservedly to the strangeness of the situation, debating nothing, accepting everything and determined to regard the supernatural as something natural. He approached the mirror, thinking he would be able to get an even clearer appreciation of the features of the image: but she remained as she had first appeared to him, very close and yet very far away, and looking like the projection, on to the inner surface of the crystal, of a figure placed so far away that human science could not measure it. The reality of what he was seeing, if one can use such a word in a circumstance like this, was evidently elsewhere, in a profound and distant and enigmatic space that is inaccessible to the living and to the edge of which the boldest thoughts hardly dare venture. Guy tried in vain to connect this figure to some terrestrial memory. For him it was entirely new and yet he seemed to recognise it. But where had he seen it? It was not in this world of earth and water.

This then was the form in which *Spirite* wanted to appear: Guy de Malivert, not knowing how to refer to the apparition he had glimpsed in the mirror, had christened her with this name, until such time as he knew what name suited her better. Before long it seemed to him that the image was losing its colour and was fading into the depths of the mirror. There was no longer anything to be seen except a kind of faint vapour of a breath, and then even this was gone. The end of the apparition was marked by the sudden reflection of a golden picture frame which hung on the opposite wall; the mirror had taken on its reflective properties once more.

When he was quite sure that the apparition would not return, at least not that evening and in that way, Guy threw himself into his armchair. Although the clock had just struck two in the morning and its silvery tones were advising him to go to bed, he could not persuade himself to do so. Yet he felt tired. This new kind of emotion, these first steps taken outside the real world, had brought about the kind of nervous lassitude that chases sleep away. Later, when he did fall asleep, he was afraid he might miss seeing Spirite if she showed herself.

With his feet stretched out on the fireguard in front of the fireplace, which had rekindled of its own accord, Guy reflected on what had happened, the feasibility of which he would surely have denied just two days ago. He dreamt of that charming head, which recalled the beautiful women glimpsed through the magic of dreams, the imagination of poets and the genius of painters, only to dismiss them as mere shadows. In it were revealed a thousand inexpressible examples of her sweetness, a thousand charms which neither nature nor art could bring together in one individual. This sample augured well for those living beyond this world. Then he asked himself what strange empathy, what mysterious and so far unconfessed affinity could attract this angel, this sylph-like creature, this soul, this spirit, to him from the depths of infinity. He still did not know what she was or in which immaterial order she should be classified. He did not dare flatter himself that he had inspired love in such a superior being: fatuity was not one of Malivert's faults. And yet he could not help admitting – by the sigh she had uttered, by the letter whose meaning she had changed, by the forbidding murmur in front of Madame d'Ymbercourt's door and by the remark she no doubt suggested to the Swedish baron – that Sprite seemed to feel for *him*, Guy de Malivert, a mere mortal, a totally feminine sentiment, which in this world would have been called jealousy. What he understood immediately, however, was that he was madly, desperately and irrevocably in love, overcome quite suddenly by a passion which eternity would not assuage.

From this moment on, all the women he had known were struck from his memory. When Spirite had appeared he had forgotten earthly love, as Romeo forgets Rosalind when he sees Juliette. Had he been Don Juan, three thousand charming names would have struck themselves from his notebook. It was not without a certain sense of terror that he felt himself bathed in this sudden flame which devoured any ideas, any willpower, any resistance and left only love alive in his soul. But it was too late. He was no longer his own master. The baron de Féroë had been right. It is a formidable thing for a living being to cross the barriers of life and to embark on an adventure as a solid body amongst the shadows, without holding the golden branch that controls the phantoms.

A terrible idea crossed Malivert's mind. If Spirite took it

into her head not to reappear, by what means would he bring her back? And if these means did not exist how would he be able to bear the darkness of the sun, having for one instant contemplated true light? A feeling of immense sadness enveloped his whole being and he fell into a state of extreme depression; for a moment that lasted an eternity he felt an awful sense of despair. This supposition was not supported by a single shred of evidence but it brought tears to his eyes, where they welled up between his eyelashes. Though he made every effort to contain them and was ashamed of his own weakness, they finally overflowed and ran slowly down his cheeks. As he was crying, he felt a mixture of surprise and delight as he sensed a veil, thinner than the lightest fabric, thinner even than woven air or spun wind, passing over his face like a caress and drying, or rather drinking, the bitter teardrops. The touch of a dragonfly's wing would not have been more delicate. It was no illusion, for the contact was repeated three times and when his tears had dried, Malivert thought he saw a diaphanous white flake, like a little cloud in the sky, melt into the shadows.

This attentive and tender show of sympathy meant Malivert could not doubt that Spirite, who seemed always to be fluttering around him, was answering his call and finding, with the lucidity of her superior being, simple ways of communicating. Spirite could enter the world in which he lived, at least as far as a soul can mix with living people. He, the mortal, was forbidden by the burdensome constraints of the flesh from pursuing her into the realm of the ideal, where she moved about. To say that Malivert went from feeling the darkest despair to feeling the purest joy will surprise no one. If, ten times in one day, a mere mortal can send you down to hell and back up to heaven, and inspire in you first the notion of blowing your brains out and then the notion of buying a villa on the shores of Lake Como as an eternal shelter for your blissful happiness, you can well imagine that the emotions inspired by a spirit must be of a totally different intensity.

Guy's passion for Spirite might seem rather sudden but

one must remember that love is often conceived at first sight. A woman spied from afar in a box at the theatre is not very different from the reflection of a soul spotted in a mirror. Many serious passions have just this kind of beginning. Besides, Guy might have been unaware of it, but this love was less sudden than it seemed. Spirite had been circling within Guy's atmospheric environment for a long time. Though he suspected nothing, she had been preparing his soul for supernatural communication: suggesting thoughts to him that punctuated the frivolity of his society existence and went beyond shallow appearances; creating in him a nostalgic ideal by conjuring up confused memories of superior worlds; diverting him from shallow love affairs and giving him a foreboding of a happiness which this earth could not give him. It was she who had broken all the strings that had been tightened around Malivert; she who had broken all the beginnings of webs woven about him; she who revealed to him the absurdity or perfidiousness of such and such a casual mistress; and she who had to this day kept his soul free of unbreakable commitments. She had stopped him on the verge of the irremediable, for though Guy's existence had experienced no event of appreciable significance from a human point of view, it was approaching a decisive time; the scales of mystery were weighing up his destiny; and this is what had persuaded Spirite to come out of the shadows which shrouded her secret protection of Guy and manifest herself to him; it was no longer enough to direct him through occult influence. What was the motivation behind her interest? Were Spirite's actions spontaneous or was she obeying an order emanating from that radiant sphere where one is *able* to do what one *wants* to do, as Dante says? That was something only she was in a position to reveal; and perhaps it will not be long before she does reveal it.

Malivert finally went to bed and quickly fell asleep. His sleep was light, transparent and filled with wonderfully dazzling images which did not have the character of dreams, but far more resembled a vision. Vast expanses of blue opened out before his closed eyes and streaks of light cut valleys of silver and gold that were lost in limitless perspective; then this picture disappeared, leaving him to look in far greater depth at blinding phosphorescent streams like a cascade of molten suns falling from eternity into infinity. The cascade in turn disappeared and in its place there stretched a sky of the kind of intense luminous white which at one time clothed those who were transfigured on Mount Thabor. Against this background, which one might have thought was the greatest possible paroxysm of splendour, a surge of stars and even brighter sparks soared first here and then there. In this light, against which the most brilliant stars were made to appear black, there was the hum of perpetual evolution. From time to time, there passed before this vast expanse of illumination, like two birds in front of the disc of the sun, two spirits which were not discernible as shadows but were illuminated by a different light. Amid this swarm, Guy de Malivert thought he recognised Spirite and he was not mistaken, though she appeared just as a brilliant spot in space, a mere globule against the incandescent brightness. In provoking this dream Spirite had wanted to show herself to her admirer in her true environment. His soul, released during sleep from its corporeal ties, wallowed in this vision. For a few minutes Guy could see with his inner eye not the extraterrestrial sphere itself, contemplation of which is only granted to souls that are totally free, but a ray of light seeping out from under the poorly closed door to the unknown. It was like being in a dark street where one can see, beneath the door of a palace where the interior is illuminated, a ray of bright light suggesting the splendour of the party. Not wanting to exhaust Malivert's still too human make-up, Spirite dispelled the visions and plunged him again into the ecstasy of ordinary sleep. Guy experienced the sensation, as he fell back into a night of prosaic dreams, of being caught like a shellfish in a matrix of black marble, by dark forces of impenetrable density; then everything vanished, even this sensation, and for two hours Guy was immersed again in the non-existence from which life gushes forth, rejuvenated and refreshed.

He slept like this until ten o'clock. Jack was watching

carefully for his master to wake, and when he saw his eyes open, he pushed wide open the flap of the double door that he was holding ajar. Then he went into the room, pulled back the curtains and walked towards Malivert's bed presenting him with a silver tray on which were two letters that had just been delivered. One was from Madame d'Ymbercourt, the other from the baron de Féroë; it was the baron's that Guy opened first.

CHAPTER 6

The baron de Féroë's note contained nothing but these words: 'Has Caesar crossed the Rubicon?' Madame d'Ymbercourt's was far less brief and implied through a few tortured phrases that he should not take vague gossip seriously and that it was perhaps more compromising to break off the habit of visiting than to increase its frequency. The whole thing ended with a remark about Adelina Patti which seemed to be indicating to Malivert that a seat was reserved for him at the Italiens in box 22. There could be no doubt about Guy's great admiration for the young diva, but in his present spiritual state he would rather hear her another evening and he vowed to invent some means to avoid the rendezvous.

The human spirit has a tendency to doubt extraordinary things when the place where they happened has taken on its normal appearance once more. So when Malivert looked in broad daylight at the Venetian mirror which was tinted blue at the centre of its cut crystal frame, he wondered, when he saw nothing more than the reflection of his own face, whether this piece of polished glass really had presented him, barely a few hours ago, with the most delightful image that any mortal eye had ever contemplated. Much as his reason would have liked to attribute this celestial vision to a dream or a frenzied delusion, his heart denied his reason. Though it is very difficult to appreciate the reality of the supernatural, he felt that the whole thing was genuine and that behind the calmness of appearances, a world of mystery was stirring. Yet nothing had changed in this apartment which a short while ago had been so quiet; and visitors would have noticed nothing amiss. For Guy, however, the door of every sideboard and every wardrobe might now open on to infinity. He took the slightest sounds to be warnings and they made him tremble.

To shake off this nervous excitement, Guy resolved to go

for a long ride. He thought he sensed that Spirite's apparitions would be nocturnal; and besides, if she had to communicate with him, her fantastical omnipresence gave her the means to find him and manifest herself wherever he might be. In this love affair, if one can give that name to such vague, frail, ethereal and impalpable relationships, Malivert's role was necessarily passive. His ideal mistress could at any moment erupt into his world while he, on the other hand, was unable to follow her into the imaginary spaces she inhabited.

Two days before, it had snowed. Quite unusually for Paris, a mild wind had not melted the white blanket into the kind of cold slush that is even more horrible than the black mud around old cobbles or the yellow mire of new tarmac; instead a bitter cold had crystallised it and it crunched like crushed glass beneath the wheels of carriages and the soles of pedestrians' shoes. Grymalkin was a fine trotter and Malivert had brought back a sleigh and a full Russian harness from St Petersburg. Opportunities for sleigh riding are not frequent in our temperate climate and sportsmen seize them with enthusiasm. Guy was proud of his sleigh. It was certainly the best looked after in Paris and could quite creditably have entered the races in Neva Square. This high-speed chase through healthy icy air appealed to him. During a hard winter in Russia, he had learnt to savour the Northern pleasures of the snow and the cold; he enjoyed sliding over the white carpet that had hardly been streaked at all by the steel blades of skates, and driving a fast horse with both hands as *izvostchicks* do. He had his horse harnessed and had soon reached Place de la Concorde and the Champs-Elysées. The piste was not ready-made or edged with banks as it is at Nevski but the snow was deep enough for the sleigh to be able to speed along without the bumps being too obvious. One cannot expect a Parisian winter to match the perfection of a muscovite winter. In the Bois de Boulogne, one might have thought one was on the *Islands*: the layer of snow was so uniform and white, especially along the lanes that cross the main road where there are fewer carriages and horses. Guy de Malivert took a road through a wood of fir trees. Their blackened arms, laden with snow that the wind had not shaken off, reminded him of the strolls he had taken in Russia. He had plenty of furs and the North wind seemed to him to be just a mild zephyr compared with the air he had braved out there: that air would have turned mercury to ice.

A considerable crowd was gathering around the edge of the lake and the throng of carriages was as great as on the finest days of autumn or spring when races featuring famous horses attract curious-minded people from every stratum of society, regardless of wealth, to the Longchamp racecourse. Reclining in eight-spring barouches, beneath huge polar bear skins with scarlet scalloped edging, high society women could be seen hugging their warm sable muffs to their fur-lined satin coats. On the elaborately braided drivers' seats, coachmen from great houses sat majestically, their shoulders kept warm by fox furs, watching no less contemptuously than their mistresses, as lowly ladies passed by, driving ponies themselves that were hitched up to some excessive, preten-tious contraption. There were also many closed carriages, for in Paris the idea of travelling in a temperature of only five or six degrees seems too arctic and boreal. A number of sleighs were to be seen amongst this whole assemblage of coaches with wheels that seemed not to have anticipated the snow. But Malivert's sleigh had the edge over all the others. Russian noblemen sauntered about as happy as reindeer in the snow, deigning to give their approval of the elegant line of the *douga* and the properly attached harness straps.

It was about three o' clock and a light mist lay over the bottom of the sky like cotton wool. The delicate veins of the leafless trees stood out against the grey background, their slim branches looking like those leaves whose pulp has been removed leaving only the fibrils. A rayless sun, like a big seal of red wax, was setting through the haze. The lake was cov-ered with skaters. Two or three days of frost had thickened the ice enough for it to be able to support the weight of the crowd. The snow had been swept aside and built up around the edges, granting a view of the blackened polished surface, streaked in every direction by the sharp blades of the skates, like those mirrors in restaurants where lovers scratch their names with the edges of diamonds. Near the bank there were men hiring out skates to bourgeois amateurs, whose tumbles provided some comic relief in this winter party, this large-scale ballet of *The Prophet*. In the middle of the lake, the skating celebrities in svelte dress devoted themselves to showing off their prowess. They spun like lightning, changed direction sharply, avoided collisions, stopped dead by digging the heel of their skate blades into the ice and traced curves, spirals, figures-of-eight and letters, like those Arab horsemen who write the name of Allah on the flank of their mounts by ruffling their coats with the point of their spurs. Others pushed around fantastically ornate light-weight sleighs, carrying beautiful fur-clad ladies, who leant back and smiled at the men, drunk with speed and cold. Some men used the tips of their fingers to guide elegant young women, wearing a Russian or Hungarian-style bonnet, a jacket decorated with braided buttonholes and stripes bordered with blue fox-fur, garish skirts that were half-hitched up with fasteners and pretty polished boots with the skate straps wound around them, like the strips of cloth on a buskin. Others were racing each other, gliding along on one leg, relying on the force of their impetus and leaning forward like the images of Hippomenes and Atalanta that can be seen amongst the chestnut trees in a border at the Tuileries gardens. The way to win the race, today as in times past, would perhaps have been to drop golden apples before these Atalantas who had been dressed by Worth. But some of them were well-bred enough for a cluster of diamonds not to have stopped them for even one minute. This continuous swarm of costumes, strangely elegant and richly original, was a kind of masked ball on ice and it made for a graceful, animated and charming spectacle, worthy of the paintbrush of Watteau, Lancret or Baron. Certain groups brought to mind the designs over doors in old châteaux, depicting the Four Seasons, in which Winter is represented by gallant noblemen pushing swan-necked sleighs that carry velvet-masked marchionesses with their muffs made into postboxes for love letters. The masks, it is true, were missing from these pretty faces, painted as they were with the rosiness of the cold. But the steel-studded or jet-fringed half-veils could be brought into position when necessary.

Malivert had stopped his sleigh near the lake and was watching this entertaining and picturesque scene, whose principal actors were known to him. He knew society well enough to be able to pick out the love affairs, the intrigues and the flirtations which made this select crowd tick. It does not take long to distinguish them from the general crowd, that troop of extras packed together unwittingly to surround any spectacle with the aim of preventing the action from appearing too naked and obvious. But he contemplated all of this with eyes which would always now be disinterested. A quite charming person passed him by, who not so long ago had had a certain fondness for him; and even seeing her leaning in an intimate, caring way on the arm of a handsome skater did not inspire in him the slightest feeling of jealousy.

He soon gave free rein to Grymalkin; the horse had been stamping its hooves impatiently in the snow, so Malivert turned its head towards Paris and began to go down the path to the lake. There is always a continuous stream of carriages along here, and pedestrians can delight in seeing the same yellow-hooded berlin, garnished with its solemn dowager, reappear ten or twelve times in one hour; they can see the same little *oeil de corbeau* coupé, displaying in its window a Havana toy dog and a doe-eyed head with the same doggy hairstyle; and their delight never seems to flag.

Guy turned away and slowed his horse's pace. The noble animal might have knocked someone down: the avenue was too crowded to allow it to go at full speed. Besides it is not the done thing to travel briskly along such a well-to-do route. He saw a familiar barouche, which he would rather not have encountered, coming towards him. Madame d'Ymbercourt was quite sensitive to the cold and Guy did not think that she would be out in a temperature of only five or six degrees. In this he showed that he knew virtually nothing about women: no temperature could stop them going to a fashionable spot where style demands they be seen. And nothing was more stylish that winter than to appear at the Bois de Boulogne and do a circuit of the frozen lake. Between three and five o' clock it was a meeting place for as many famous names and personalities as the whole of Paris, to use the language of the chronicles, can gather together at a given spot. It is shameful for a woman of any standing not to see her initials mentioned amongst those of the beautiful women of the day in some well-informed gazette. Madame d'Ymbercourt was beautiful enough, rich enough and fashionable enough to believe herself obliged to conform to the dictates of fashion, and trembling a little beneath her furs, which like all French women she wore out of doors, she carried out the pilgrimage to the lake. Malivert really wanted to let Grymalkin break into a full trot. It would have liked nothing better. But Madame d'Ymbercourt had spotted him and he felt obliged to draw his sleigh up beside the countess's carriage.

He chatted with her in a general and casual manner and put forward the excuse of a grand dinner party which would finish late, so as to avoid the trip to the Italiens. Just then a sleigh brushed by his own. This sleigh was drawn by a magnificent Orloff breed with a steel-grey coat, a white mane and the kind of tail made of hair that sparkles like silver thread. Restrained by a full-bearded Russian coachman, wearing a green cloth kaftan and a fur hat trimmed with astrakhan, it showed proud indignation at being held back: it stamped its hooves and shook its head in such a way that its nostrils touched its knees. The elegance of the vehicle, the coachman's outfit and the horse's beauty attracted Guy's attention. At first he had assumed the woman sitting in the corner of the sleigh was one of those Russian princesses who come to Paris for a season or two to dazzle the city – if Paris can be dazzled by anything – with their eccentric luxury. What did he feel when he recognised, or thought he recognised in this woman, features which resembled a face he had glimpsed, a face which would always be indelibly engraved in the depths of his soul but one which he certainly did not expect to encounter in the Bois de Boulogne, after seeing it appear, like Helen to Faust, in a kind of magic mirror? The sight of her made him shiver so suddenly that Grymalkin felt the nervous shock and bolted. Casting a few words of apology towards Madame d'Ymbercourt about the impatience of his horse and his own inability to control it, Guy began to follow the sleigh which then quickened its pace.

As though she were astonished at being followed, the lady half-turned her head over her shoulder to see who it was that dared be so bold. Though this pose only showed her in what artists call half profile, Guy could make out through the black net of the veil a wavy band of golden hair, an eye the shade of midnight blue and a rose-coloured cheek so perfect that only the snow of the highest mountain tops, coloured by the setting sun, can give a vague idea of it. In the lobe of her ear a turquoise sparkled and on the portion of the nape of her neck which was visible between the collar of her fur coat and the brim of her hat there was a capricious, twisting little curl, as light as a puff of air and as fine as the hair of a child. It was definitely the apparition of the night but imbued with that degree of reality which a phantom must assume in broad daylight and near the lake in the Bois de Boulogne. How did Spirite come to be there, cloaked in this form that was so humanly charming and was no doubt visible to others besides himself? For it was difficult to believe, even if one conceded the impalpability of the apparition, that the coachman, the horse and the sleigh were ghosts. It was a question which Guy did not take the time to resolve. To reassure himself that he had not been fooled by one of those resemblances that dissolve when they are examined more closely, he wanted to get in front of the sleigh to see this mysterious face head on. He let Grymalkin go completely. And the horse set off like a shot. For a few minutes the white steam jets of its breath reached the tail end of the sleigh they were pursuing. But although Grymalkin was a fine animal, it was not strong enough to do battle with a Russian trotter that was perhaps the most handsome example of the breed that Malivert had ever seen. The kaftaned coachman made a slight clicking sound with his tongue and in a few bounding strides the steel-grey horse left Grymalkin behind, putting enough space between the two sleighs to reassure his mistress, if by any chance she was alarmed.

The lady who so closely resembled Spirite certainly did not intend to make Malivert despair in his pursuit, for her sleigh now began to travel at a more moderate speed. The race had taken the two vehicles into the avenue of firs, which was not blocked at the time by any other vehicles. Though the chase had settled down into a steady pace, Grymalkin could still not reach the Orloff trotter. When it tried its hardest, it only barely managed to keep the same distance between the one sleigh and the other. The horses' shoes threw up white flakes which were dashed into frozen dust against the shiny leather of the snow-screen. The fumes of white produced by the perspiration of the noble steeds enveloped them like actual clouds. At the far end of the avenue, which was blocked by carriages heading along the main road, the two sleighs found themselves side by side for a moment. For a few seconds Guy was able to see the face of the bogus Russian, as her veil was lifted up by the wind. A smile of heavenly malice hovered on her lips, their curve forming the same arc traced by the mouth of the Mona Lisa. Her eyes sparkled and shone blue like sapphires and a slightly rosier haze now coloured her velvet cheeks. Spirite, for it was most definitely her, lowered her veil and the coachman spurred on the animal which raced off with fearsome zeal. Guy cried out in terror for at that very moment a great berlin was crossing the path; forgetting that Spirite was an immaterial being, protected from all earthly accidents, he was expecting an appalling crash. But horse, coachman and sleigh all passed through the carriage as though through fog and Malivert soon lost them from view. Grymalkin seemed frightened, nervous shivers were making his normally sturdy legs tremble as though he could not understand the disappearance of the sleigh. Animals have mysteriously profound instincts; they see what the careless human eye often misses; and some of them seem to possess a sense of the supernatural. The horse soon calmed down again, however, as it rejoined the line of real carriages along the edge of the lake.

Going down Avenue de l'Impératrice, Guy came upon the baron de Féroë who was also returning from the woods in a light-weight *drojki*. After asking Malivert to light his cigar, the baron said to him in a half-joking, half-mysterious way: 'Madame d'Ymbercourt won't be happy; she'll cause a real scene with you this evening at the Italiens, if you're unwise enough to go there: I don't think that steeple chase in sleighs was to her taste. Tell Jack to throw a blanket over Grymalkin by the way. It could easily catch a dose of pneumonia.'

CHAPTER 7

Guy had reached the stage where strange things no longer surprised him and he did not think it utterly extraordinary that a sleigh should pass through a carriage. This ability to go through obstacles into which vehicles of this earth would have crashed clearly illustrated that this was a fantastical team of horses, which had come from the stables of the mist and could drive only Spirite. Spirite was evidently jealous or at least, as all her actions indicated, she wanted to separate Malivert from Madame d'Ymbercourt. Her way of going about it was probably the right one, for as Guy came off the round-about at the Etoile he saw the countess in her barouche; she seemed to be listening quite indulgently to the undoubtedly kind words which were being addressed to her by Monsieur d'Aversac as he leant gallantly over the withers of his walking horse.

'This is revenge for the sleigh,' said Malivert to himself. 'But I'm not one to take offence easily. D'Aversac is a pseudo-intellectual, just as Madame d'Ymbercourt is a bogus beauty. They are perfectly suited. I can pass judgement on them in a totally disinterested way since the affairs of this world no longer concern me. They would make 'a well-matched husband and wife', to quote some song or other.'

This was the result of Madame d'Ymbercourt's ploy. Having spotted Guy, she had leant over the edge of the barouche, a little further than was perhaps proper, to respond to Monsieur d'Aversac's pleasantries. The poor countess thought she could attract her half-hearted admirer by smarting his ego. She had only glimpsed Spirite's appearance but had guessed she was a formidable rival. Ordinarily Guy was so calm and his eagerness to pursue this mysterious sleigh and this woman whom no one had ever seen at the Bois de Boulogne, had wounded her deeply: she had not been fooled by his hurried excuse and she did not believe that Grymalkin had bolted. D'Aversac, who was not used to being treated so well, was holding his head high with joy. He modestly attributed to his own merit something he would have been wiser to explain as feminine pique. In his magnanimity he even felt sorry for poor Malivert for being too confident of Madame d'Ymbercourt's affection. It is easy to imagine all the plans that this gentleman's self-conceit – encouraged by a semblance of affection – enjoyed hatching on the basis of this little occurrence.

That day Guy was dining in town, at a house where it was difficult to turn down an invitation which had been extended to him well in advance. Thankfully there were a great many guests and no one noticed how preoccupied he was. When the meal was over, he exchanged a few words with the mistress of the house, and once his presence had been sufficiently noticed, he negotiated a skilful retreat towards the second drawing room. There he shook hands with the eminent men of his acquaintance who had retired to discuss things of an important or confidential nature more freely. Then he disappeared and headed for his club where he thought he might meet the baron de Féroë. And indeed he did find him, sitting at a small table covered with green baize. He was playing écarté with the beaming d'Aversac, who in fairness was trying to hide his private joy so as not to humiliate Malivert. Contrary to the proverb, 'Lucky at cards, unlucky in love', d'Aversac was winning, and however unsuperstitious he was, this ought to have inspired in him a degree of doubt as to the legitimacy of his hopes. Since, when the game was over, the baron was losing, he was able to get up, claiming he was tired, and gallantly refuse the chance for revenge which his opponent was offering him. The baron de Féroë and Guy de Malivert left together and went for a stroll down the boulevard that runs alongside the club.

'What will the regulars at that salon they call the Bois de Boulogne be thinking of that woman, that sleigh and that coachman?' said Guy to the baron. 'They were so fantastically remarkable and yet no one knows them.'

'The vision was only made manifest to you, and the countess upon whom the spirit wanted to exert an influence, and me, who in my role as one of the initiated, can see what is imperceptible to the rest of humanity. You can be sure that if Madame d'Ymbercourt talks about the beautiful Russian princess and the magnificent trotter, people won't know what she means.'

'Do you think,' said Malivert to the baron, 'that I will see Spirite again soon?'

'Expect a visit imminently,' replied Monsieur de Féroë. 'My extraterrestrial sources inform me that they are paying you a lot of attention out there.'

'Will it be tonight or tomorrow?' cried Malivert with the impatience of a lover greedy for passion or a neophyte keen to uncover a mystery. 'Will it be at home or somewhere unexpected, as happened today?'

'I couldn't tell you precisely,' replied the Swedish baron. 'The spirits, for whom time does not exist or has ceased to exist, have no hours as they live immersed in eternity. For Spirite, it would be no different if she saw you this evening or in a thousand years. However, the spirits who deign to enter into communication with the rest of us poor mortals are aware of the brevity of our lives and of the imperfection and fragility of our organs. They know that, measured on an eternal scale, the time between one apparition and the next would be sufficient for the perishable shell of man to turn one hundred times to dust. Spirite will probably not leave you languishing. She has come down into our sphere and seems determined not to return to hers until her task is accomplished.'

'But what is this task,' said Malivert. 'If nothing of the supernatural world is closed off from you, you must know the motive that guides this pure spirit towards a being which is still subject to the conditions of life.'

'On that point, my dear Guy,' replied the baron de Féroë, 'my lips are sealed; the secret of the spirits must not be passed on. I was warned to put you on your guard against any seduction on earth and to stop you forming ties which could perhaps chain your soul to a place where it would eternally regret not being more free. My mission goes no further than that.'

Conversing in this way, Malivert and the baron, with their carriages following them along the avenue at a walking pace, arrived at the Madeleine. Its Greek colonnade looked silver in the pale winter moonlight and at the end of the wide Rue Royale it looked like the Parthenon – an appearance which the light of day dispels. Having arrived here, the two friends parted and climbed back into their coupés.

When Malivert got home, he threw himself into his armchair, leant his elbow on the table and began to dream. Spirite's apparition in the mirror had inspired in him that immaterial kind of desire, that winged will-power, to which the sight of an angel gives birth. But her presence by the lake in a more truly feminine form awakened all the ardour of human love in his heart. He felt himself bathed in a passionate fragrance and consumed with the kind of absolute love that even eternal possession cannot satisfy. As he was dreaming with his fist stretched out on the table, covered with papers, he saw a hand taking shape against the dark background of the Turkish carpet. The perfection of this narrow, elongated hand has never been equalled by art and it would be useless for nature even to attempt to attain it. It was a diaphanous hand with slender fingers, and nails that gleamed like onyx. The surface of the back of the hand let a few azure veins show through; they looked like those blueish highlights which make the milky composition of opal so iridescent. But it was not the lamplight that illuminated them. The pink freshness of its colour and the perfect delicacy of its form meant this could only be the hand of Spirite. The slim wrist was shapely, casual and full of breeding, and it disappeared into a haze of loose-fitting lace. So as to make it clear that the hand was only there as a sign, the arm and the body were missing. As Guy watched it, his eyes no longer astonished by extraordinary occurrences, the fingers of the hand stretched out over one of the sheets of writing paper which were strewn in confusion over the table and simulated the movements necessary for writing. They seemed to be forming lines and when they had covered the whole page with a degree of speed typical of an actor writing a letter in some comic scene, Guy took hold of the sheet of paper, thinking he would find some written phrases or some familiar or unfamiliar symbols. The paper was completely blank. Guy looked at the sheet and appeared quite disconcerted. He held it up to the lamp, scrutinised it from every angle and in every light without discovering the slightest trace of written characters. Yet the hand continued the same imaginary task on another sheet, and with no apparent result.

'What is the meaning of this game?' Guy wondered. 'Might it be that Spirite has written with invisible ink that has to be held near the fire for the characters she has traced to be made visible? But her mysterious fingers are not holding a pen, nor even the shadow of a pen. What can this mean? Must I myself act as secretary to the spirit and be my own *medium*, to use the accepted expression? They say spirits that can produce illusions and apparitions and conjure up frightening or wonderful images in the minds of those they obsess are incapable of influencing material reality; they couldn't even lift a feather.'

He remembered how he had felt driven to write the note to Madame d'Ymbercourt and he thought that Spirite might manage to dictate to his inner self what she wanted to say through a nerve impulse. All he had to do was relax his hand and silence his own ideas as far as possible, so as not to mix them up with those of the spirit. Gathering himself together, and isolating himself from the outside world, Guy imposed silence on the tumult of his overexcited brain. He turned up the wick of his lamp slightly. Then he took a pen laden with ink, put his hand on a piece of paper and, with his heart beating full of fearful hope, he waited.

After a few minutes, Guy experienced a strange sensation. It seemed to him that his personality was leaving him, that his own memories were being erased like those of a confused dream and that his ideas were disappearing out of sight like birds that vanish in the sky. Although his body was still near the table in the same position, Guy's inner self was absent; it had faded and disappeared. Another soul, or at least another mind, was exchanging itself for his own and was taking command of those servants that await the order of the unknown master before taking any action. The nerves in his fingers trembled and began to make movements of which he was unaware; the nib of his pen began to race over the paper, rapidly forming symbols in Guy's hand, though slightly modified by an alien force. This is what Spirite dictated to her medium. This extraterrestrial confession was discovered amongst Malivert's papers and we have been granted permission to transcribe it.

Spirite's Dictation

It is necessary first of all that you should know the identity of the being you cannot define that has slipped into your existence. However perceptive you might be, you could never manage to work out its true nature. So, as in a badly written tragedy where the hero has to give his own name, status and testimonials, I too am obliged to give my own explanations. I do, however, have the excuse that no one else could do it in my place. Your intrepid heart, which did not hesitate to answer my appeal to become involved in the mysterious terrors of the unknown, does not need reassurances. And besides, any danger which might exist would not stop you pursuing the adventure. This invisible world, for which reality is a veil, has its pitfalls and its chasms but you will not fall into them. The spirits of falsehood and depravity are everywhere; there are angels of darkness just as there are angels of light; rebellious powers just as there are subdued powers; salutary forces and harmful forces. The bottom of the mystical ladder, whose top thrusts deep into eternal light, is besieged by darkness. I hope that with my help you will climb the rungs of enlightenment. I am neither an angel nor a demon, nor one of those mediating spirits that transmit divine will through infinity, in the way that the nervous system communicates human will to the limbs of the body. I am just a soul still waiting to be judged. Celestial goodness, however, has led me to believe that I will receive a favourable sentence. So, having inhabited your earth, I might say, like the shepherd's melancholic epitaph in the picture by Poussin: *Et in Arcadia ego*. Don't let this Latin quotation make you think I am the soul of a literary woman. In the environment where I am, one has a sense of intuition about everything and the various languages spoken by the human race, before and after the scattering of Babel, are all equally familiar to us. Words are merely the shadow of the idea and we possess the idea itself in its essential state. If there were such a thing as age in my new homeland, where time has ceased to exist, I would be extremely young. Very few days have passed since I was set free by death and left the atmosphere you breathe. Now I have been brought back by a feeling which the transition from one world to the other has done nothing to erase. My life on earth, or rather my last appearance on your planet, was extremely brief. But I had time enough to experience the most painful things a tender soul can feel. When the baron de Féroë was trying to establish the nature of the spirit, whose vague manifestations were troubling you, he asked you if a woman or a girl had ever died of love for you; and he was nearer to the truth than he thought. Although your memories could not call anything to mind, because you were unaware of it, the assertion profoundly moved your soul and your agitation was poorly concealed beneath a sceptical and spirited denial.

Without your noticing, my existence passed close to yours. Your eyes were focussed elsewhere. And I stayed in the shadows of your life.

The first time I saw you was in the parlour at the convent des Oiseaux. You had come to visit your sister, who like me was a boarder there. She was in a higher year, though. I was only thirteen or fourteen at the very most and I didn't look my age. I was so delicate and sweet and fair. You paid no attention to that little girl, that child who munched away at the Marquis praline chocolate her mother had brought her, and at the same time shot you a furtive sideways glance. You must have been twenty or twenty-two then and in my childish naivety I thought you very handsome. The kind, affectionate way you spoke to your sister both touched me and seduced me and I wished I had a brother like you. My girlish imagination went no further. When Mademoiselle de Malivert's studies were over, she was removed from the convent and you never came back. But the image of you was never erased from my memory. It was preserved on the white vellum of my soul, just like a faint but skilful line drawing, found again after a long time: almost invisible but still there, the only vestige of a vanished being. The notion that such a great individual might have noticed me when I was still a junior and when more advanced boarders treated me with a sort of disdain, would have been asking far too much and it didn't even occur to me, at least not at the time. But I thought about you extremely often and in those chaste novels which fill the dreams of the most innocent imaginations, it was always you who played the role of the Prince Charming; it was you who saved me from fantastical dangers, you who carried me off through underground passages, and you who chased off the pirates and the bandits and took me back to my father, the king. For such a hero, I had at least to be an infanta or a princess and modestly I took on that identity. At other times, the novel became a portrayal of country life. You were a shepherd, I was a shepherdess, and our flocks mingled in a pasture of sweetest green. Though you suspected nothing, you had assumed an important position in my life and you were the sovereign master. I came to you with little scholastic successes and I worked as hard as I could to deserve your approbation. I told myself: 'He doesn't know I've won a prize, but if he did, he'd be happy.' And though I was naturally lazy, I set to work again with renewed energy. It's strange, isn't it, that a child could secretly give her soul to a master of her choice, perceive herself as his humble servant, and all the time he didn't even suspect that faithful homage? Don't you think it even stranger, though, that this initial impression never faded? For it lasted a whole, pitifully short lifetime and continues beyond it. When I saw you, something indefinable and mysterious shivered within me. I only understood the meaning of this when my eyes shut and then opened for ever. My state of impalpability, the fact that I am a pure spirit, means that now I may tell you these things, things that a girl on earth might hide. But the immaculate innocence of a soul cannot blush; celestial propriety admits love.

Two years went by and I had grown from a child into a girl. My dreams were starting to become a little less childlike, though they retained their innocence: they were no longer infused with so much pink and blue and didn't always finish in an illuminated apotheosis. I often went to the foot of the garden to sit on a bench, far from my companions, who were busy playing games or having whispered conversations. I would murmur the syllables of your name like a kind of litany. Sometimes, though, I was bold enough to think that name might become mine. It would either happen as the result of some stroke of fate or else it would follow a tangle of adventures, like a cloak-and-dagger mystery, whose plot I concocted according to my whim.

My family was on a par with yours and my parents enjoyed sufficient wealth and status for it to be clear that this distant project of marriage, which I was conceiving in the most secret recess of my heart, was not just a pipedream or a mad ambition. Nothing would have been more natural than to come upon you one day in an environment to which we both had access. Would you like me though? Would you think me pretty? It was a question to which the little mirror I had as a boarder never answered no. That is something you can judge for yourself, now that you have seen the reflection I sent to your Venetian mirror and my apparition at the Bois de Boulogne. What if you paid no more attention to the girl than to the child at the convent des Oiseaux? This thought filled me with profound despair. But youth is never despondent for long and my imagination soon became more cheerful again. It seemed impossible to me that when you saw me you wouldn't recognise that I was your conquest and that I belonged to you. I was the soul marked with your seal, the woman who since childhood had devoted herself to adoring you, quite simply the woman created expressly for you. I didn't express this to myself so clearly; the impulses of my heart weren't illuminated then as they are now that I can see both sides of life; but I had a profound instinct, blind faith and an irresistible feeling. Despite my virginal ignorance and a candour which maybe no one else took to such extremes, I had in my soul a passion which was to consume me; it is revealed today for the first time. I hadn't made any friends at the convent and I lived alone with the thought of you. I was very protective of my secret and dreaded pouring my heart out or confiding in someone. Any relationship which would have distracted me from my sole interest I found repellent. People called me 'the serious one' and the schoolmistresses put me forward as a good example.

I awaited the date set for my leaving the convent with less eagerness than might be supposed; being there did at least give me some respite between thinking and making a move.

As long as I was shut up behind those high walls I was quite justified in deluding myself idly in my dreams, without having to reproach myself in the slightest. Once I had flown the cage, however, I had to direct my flight, head for my goal and ascend towards my star. But traditions, morals, propriety, the infinite dictates of decorum and the ever thickening veils with which civilisation surrounds everything, forbid a girl from making the first move in affairs of the heart. She is not allowed to do anything to reveal herself to her ideal. A justifiable sense of pride opposes what she has to offer, which itself must be priceless. Her eyes must remain lowered, her lips still, her bosom motionless. No hint of blushing or paleness must betray her when she comes face to face with the secret object of her love, who will often wander off, thinking her disdainful or indifferent. But for a word, a glance or a smile, how many souls that were made for one another have followed diverging paths that take them further and further apart and make their relationship impossible for ever? How many appallingly wasted existences have owed their unhappiness to a similar cause, of which everyone is unaware, sometimes even the victims themselves? I had often had thoughts like this and they came more forcefully to mind when I was about to leave the convent and go into society. I kept my resolve, however. The day came for me to leave. My mother came to fetch me and I said my goodbyes to my companions with only a moderate burst of feeling. I left no friendships and no memories within those walls, where several years of my life had passed by. The thought of you was my only treasure.

CHAPTER 8

It was with an intense feeling of joy that I entered the room, or rather the little apartment, which my mother had prepared for my coming out of the convent des Oiseaux. It consisted of a bedroom, a big dressing room and a drawing room with windows looking out on to a garden, itself enlarged by the view of adjoining gardens. A low wall, completely covered with a thick curtain of ivy, served as a boundary. Stone was nowhere to be seen. There was just a succession of ancient trees – gigantic chestnuts that gave the impression of a boundless park. It was barely possible, even in the far distance, to pick out, amongst the furthest clumps of vegetation, the corner of a roof or the strange kink of a chimney pipe, a signature that Paris adds at the bottom of all its horizons. It is a rare pleasure, and one reserved for the wealthy, to have an outlook on to a wide, free and hazy expanse of air, sky, sun and greenery in the middle of the city. It is rather unpleasant, is it not, to sense other existences, passions, vices and unhappiness too close at hand? And is the tender modesty of the soul not a little crushed by being so close to such things? So I experienced a true feeling of joy when I looked through my windows at that oasis of freshness, silence and solitude. It was August, for I had just finished my last school year at the convent, and the foliage still retained all its verdant intensity, though with the warmer tone which the passage of summer lends to vegetation. In the middle of the flower-bed that was laid out beneath my windows, a clump of geraniums in full flower dazzled the eyes with scarlet fireworks. Their redness was really brighter than fire and it was made to appear all the more so by the emerald green velvet carpet of English rye grass that formed the lawn around the flower-bed. The path of fine sand had been made to shimmer like a ribbon by the teeth of the rake. And the birds skipped along it confidently, looking quite at home. I resolved to join them in a stroll but without making them fly off.

My room was hung with white cashmere divided up by cords of blue silk. This too was the colour of the furniture and the curtains. In my little drawing room, which was decorated in the same way, a magnificent Erard piano presented its keyboard to my hands and I immediately tested its mellow tone. A rosewood bookcase, placed opposite the piano, contained those pure books, those chaste poets, which a virgin can read. Its lower shelves were home to the scores of the great composers: Bach stood shoulder to shoulder with Haydn; Mozart was next to Beethoven; Raphael was near Michelangelo; and Meyerbeer leant on Weber. My mother had collected the composers I admired, my favourite masters. An elegant jardinière full of sweet-scented flowers bloomed in the centre of the room like an enormous bouquet. I was being treated like a spoilt child. I was an only daughter and all my parents' affection was naturally concentrated on me.

I was to make my début in society at the beginning of the season in two or three months' time. That is when the holidays, the trips, the visits to spa towns and gambling resorts, the stays at châteaux, the hunts and the races, all come to an end; as does everything that polite society invents to pass the time. It is not decent for well-bred people to spend this period in Paris. Business had kept my parents there that year and I was happier staying in the city than going to the miserable old château in the depths of Brittany where I often went during the holidays. Besides, I thought I would get the chance to meet you, to hear about you, or to come across people you knew. However, I found out indirectly that you had left a long time before to travel to Spain and the trip was due to last several months more. Your friends, to whom you wrote only rarely, did not expect you until winter; they claimed you were caught up with some mantilla-clad Spanish girl over there. This news I found only slightly worrying and despite my modesty I was proud enough to think my golden coils of hair could do battle with all the jet plaits in Andalusia. I also discovered that you wrote for the reviews using the Latinised pseudonym of one of the names, known only to your close friends, with which you were baptised; and that the perfect gentleman in you concealed a distinguished writer. With an understandable sense of curiosity, I searched through the collection of newspapers for all the articles signed in this way. To read a writer's work is to communicate with his soul; a book is a way, is it not, of confiding in an ideal friend and conversing with someone who is absent? One must not always take everything an author says at face value: one must bear in mind philosophical or literary systems, the affectations of contemporary fashion, or the fact that reticence might have been necessary, that a style might have been deliberately chosen or imposed or that it might be a reverential imitation; one must bear in mind anything that can alter the surface mould of a writer. Beneath all these disguises, however, the true attitude of the soul is ultimately revealed to anyone who knows how to read. Sincere thoughts are often to be found between the lines. And the poet's secret, which he does not always want to surrender to the masses, can eventually be divined. One after another the veils fall away and the words of the enigmas are revealed. To get an idea of what you were like, I made an extremely attentive study of the travel writing, the novellas and the pieces of philosophy, criticism and verse, which were published here and there, separated by lengthy intervals, marking the various phases of your spirit. It is less difficult to become acquainted with a subjective author than with an objective one: the former expresses his feelings, puts forward his ideas and judges society and creation according to an ideal; the latter portrays objects as nature presents them, proceeding with images and descriptions, bringing things before the reader's eyes, drawing and clothing and colouring his characters precisely, putting words they would really have said into their mouths and reserving judgement. This was the way you wrote. At first sight, someone might have accused you of a certain disdainful impartiality. You drew little distinction between a lizard and a man or between the redness of a setting sun and a city on fire. On closer inspection, it was possible to detect, in sudden outbursts and sharp surges that were cut

100

short, a profound sensitivity held back by an elevated sense of decency which did not want its emotions to show.

This literary analysis accorded with the instinctive judgement of my heart. And now that nothing is hidden from me, I know how right I was. Any sentimental, tearful and hypocritically virtuous pomposity appalled you and you considered deceiving the soul to be the worst of crimes. This notion made you extremely sober when expressing tender or passionate thoughts. You preferred silence to lies or exaggeration about those sacred things. So much so that you must have seemed unfeeling, hard and even a little cruel in the eyes of some fools. I understood all that, and didn't doubt the kindness of your heart for a moment. There could be no uncertainty as to the nobility of your spirit: your proud disdain for vulgarity, platitude, envy and all moral ugliness illustrated it sufficiently. Through reading your work, I acquired a knowledge of you equal to any that everyday intimacy could lead to; and I had only seen you once. I had penetrated into the most secret recesses of your mind. I knew your points of reference, your aims, your motives, what you liked and what you disliked, what you admired and what you were disgusted by, your whole intellectual personality in fact, and from that I deduced your character. Sometimes as I read, I would be struck by a passage that was a revelation for me and I would get up and go to the piano and play a tune of equivalent colour and sentiment, as a kind of commentary on your remark. This would prolong its effect with ringing melancholic vibrations. I liked to hear the echo of your idea in another of the arts. Perhaps those links were imaginary and could not have been seized upon by anyone else but me, but some of them were certainly real. And this I know, now that I live at the eternal source of inspiration and can see it falling in luminous sparks on to the heads of geniuses.

As I read those of your works I could procure – for the scope of a young girl's movement is so limited that the simplest procedure becomes difficult for her – the season was advancing and the treetops were turning bronze with tints of saffron in the fullness of autumn. The leaves detached them-

101

selves one by one from the branches and despite all the gardener's care and attention, he could not stop the sand and the lawn from becoming half hidden. Sometimes as I walked in the garden beneath the chestnut trees, a chestnut fell on my head like a ball, or one rolled at my feet, its husk split open. This interrupted my dreams and made me tremble involuntarily. The delicate plants and the shrubs that were sensitive to the cold were put back into the greenhouse. The birds began to look worried as they do when winter is coming and in the evenings we could hear them quarrelling through the leaf-stripped boughs. The season was at last about to begin. The handsome, the elegant and the rich were returning to Paris from every point on the horizon. Solemn carriages with panels emblazoned with coats of arms started to be seen again on the Champs-Elysées, driving slowly up towards the Arc de l'Etoile to catch the last ray of sunshine. The Théâtre-Italien publicised the listings of its singers, its programme of events and its forthcoming opening in all the newspapers. I was overjoyed at the idea that everyone returning would bring you back from Spain, that you would be weary of climbing the Sierras, and would quite enjoy appearing at the balls and parties and meetings where I hoped to encounter you.

When I went to the Bois de Boulogne with my mother, I saw you pass by our carriage on your horse but so swiftly that I hardly had time to recognise you. This was the first time I had seen you since your visit to the convent des Oiseaux. All the blood rushed to my heart; it was like an electric shock. Pretending to be cold, I lowered my veil to hide the change in my expression and retreated silently into the corner of the coupé. My mother pushed the window up and said, 'It's not very warm. The fog is starting to gather. We'll go home unless you want to continue the drive.' I made a sign of acceptance. I had seen what I wanted to see; I knew that you were in Paris.

One day a week we had a box at the Italiens. It was a great treat for me to go and hear the singers: I had read so many eulogies about them but I knew nothing of them myself.

Another hope gently stirred my heart too: I don't need to tell you what it was. The day came. They were putting on *La Somnambula* and La Patti was to sing. Mother had had me dressed in a simple, charming way that suited my age: I wore a layer of white taffeta underneath, covered by a muslin dress with pearl knots and blue velvet bows. My hair was done up in a velvet hair band of the same colour, the ends of which hung down on to my shoulders. This was surrounded by a twist of pearls. As I was looking at myself in my dressing-table mirror and the maid was putting the final touches to her creation, I said to myself: 'Does he like blue? In Alfred de Musset's *Le Caprice*, Madame de Léry claims it is a silly colour.' But I couldn't help thinking this blue ribbon suited my fair hair. If you had seen me, I think you would have liked me. 'Mademoiselle is very pretty this evening,' Clotilde the maid said, as she puffed out the folds of my skirt and adjusted some of the bows on my bodice.

The carriage deposited my mother and me in front of the colonnade; my father was to join us later. Slowly we began to climb the great staircase, its steps covered with red carpet. Enveloped in a warm atmosphere of vetiver and patchouli, some women still had all their finery hidden beneath coats, furs, burnous, scarves and ball capes, which they would leave in the arms of the valets. They climbed the stairs trailing lengths of flowing moiré, satin and velvet behind them; and they rested the tips of their fingers on the arms of solemn men in white ties whose black tailcoats, with their rows of medals on the lapels, indicated that they intended to go on to some official or diplomatic party after leaving the Italiens. Slim, slender young people with centre partings and the most perfect elegance followed a few steps behind, connected to the group by a smile.

There is nothing new about all of this, I'm sure, and you would paint a better picture of it than I can. But it was a totally new spectacle for a little boarding-school pupil making her début in society. Life is always the same; it is a play in which only the audience changes; but those who haven't seen the play are fascinated by it as though it were made just for them and were being put on for the first time. I was cheerful and I felt beautiful. Some approving eyeglasses were focussed on me and some women had turned their heads away after quickly looking me up and down and finding nothing that could be improved upon in my person or in my dress.

A secret premonition told me I would see you that evening. And this hope gave my features a slightly animated appearance and brought a brighter shade than usual to my cheeks. We settled ourselves in our box and the opera-glasses soon turned to fix their attention on me. I was a new face and that gets noticed at the Théâtre-Italien. It is a kind of giant salon where everybody knows everybody else. My mother's presence made it clear who I was and when heads inclined towards one another I realised that I was being talked about in several boxes and in a favourable light no doubt, for benevolent smiles followed the whispered remarks. It embarrassed me a little to be the focus of people's attention; it was the first time I had worn a low-cut dress and I could feel my shoulders shiver beneath the semi-transparent chiffon which covered them. People had paid very little attention to the overture and it was the curtain rising that turned their heads towards the stage. This brought an end to my embarrassment. This beautiful room studded with diamonds and flowers, with its gilt, its lights and its white caryatids, had certainly inspired in me an unexpected sense of admiration and surprise; and Bellini's music, played by first-class musicians, carried me away into an enchanted world. For me, though, this was not the truly interesting aspect of the show. As my ears listened to the Sicilian maestro's mellow arias, my eyes made a furtive study of each box, running over the balcony and combing the rows of the stalls in my attempt to find you. You only arrived towards the end of the first act and once the curtain had come down you turned around towards the auditorium. You seemed quite bored as you gazed vaguely at the boxes without focussing your opera-glasses on anyone in particular. Your face was tanned by the six months you had spent in Spain and there was something nostalgic about your expression, as though you were missing the country you'd just left behind. My heart was beating extremely hard as you made this rapid inspection. For a moment I thought your eyes had stopped on me; but I was mistaken. I saw you leave your seat and reappear a few moments later in a box opposite ours. It was occupied by a pretty woman, lavishly turned out, with black hair that shone like satin, and a pale pink dress that almost blended into the flesh colour of her bosom. Diamonds sparkled on her head, in her ears, around her neck and on her arms. Next to her opera-glasses on the velvet ledge there blossomed a bouquet of violets and camellias. Further back in the shadows, I could make out an elderly character, bald and obese and wearing a tailcoat that half hid an exotic medal. The lady spoke to you with evident pleasure and you replied in a calm, detached manner, without appearing particularly flattered by her over-friendly behaviour. My annoyance at not having been noticed by you was countered by the joy of sensing that you didn't like this woman, with her bold eyes, her provocative smile and her sparkling outfit.

After a few minutes, as the instruments were beginning to tune up for the second act, you left the lady with the diamonds and the old man with the medal and returned to your seat. The performance ended without your having turned your head, and in my soul I experienced a sort of surge of impatience against you. I was astonished that you hadn't guessed that a young girl in a white dress embellished with blue had a strong desire to be noticed by the gentleman whom she had secretly chosen for herself. I had hoped for such a long time to find myself in the same place as you. This wish had been granted and you didn't even have any idea I was there. It seemed to me that you ought to have felt a shiver of empathy, turned and looked slowly around the auditorium for the cause of this inner disquiet, brought your gaze to rest on my box, held your hand to your heart and gone into raptures. The hero of a novel would not have failed to do this; but you were not the hero of a novel.

My father was detained by a grand dinner and only arrived half-way through the second act. Seeing you in the stalls, he said, 'Guy de Malivert is over there; I didn't know he was back from Spain. His trip will be good material for a fair few bullfights in the *Revue*; Guy is a little barbaric, after all.' I liked hearing your name come from my father's lips. You weren't unknown to my family and it would have been quite possible, and even easy, to organise an introduction. This idea consoled me a little for the lack of success of my evening. The performance came to an end without further incident, other than the shower of bouquets, the encores and the ovations for La Patti. As we waited down below in the vestibule for the servant to come and announce that the carriage was ready, I saw you go past with a friend and take a cigar out of a case of fine Manila esparto. Your desire to smoke had made you oblivious, it must be said, to the display of beautiful and, admittedly, ugly women who had gathered on the lower steps of the staircase. You threaded your way through this mass of material without being too concerned about ruffling any of it and you had soon reached the door, leaving your friend to walk through the furrow you had opened up.

When I got home, I was both happy and discontented. I went to bed after vaguely attempting to play some of the tunes from *La Somnambula*, as though to prolong the vibration of the evening. I fell asleep thinking about you.

CHAPTER 9

When, after a certain period of time, one confronts the memory of something with the image, it is often the case that the imagination has worked like a painter who carries on with a portrait in the absence of the model. He softens the straight lines, blends the hues, blurs the contours and despite himself guides the specimen back to his own notion of the ideal. I had not seen you for more than three years, but my heart had kept an exact record of your features. It was just that you looked less like my memory of you. Your face had acquired character and confidence and the tan from your travels had given your complexion a warmer and more robust hue. The man within the young man was becoming clearer and you had this air of calm authority and self-confident strength which is perhaps more appealing to women than good looks. I kept this first drawing of you in the depths of my soul, this faint but indelible sketch of the individual who was to exert so much influence on me: it was no less precious to me than a miniature of a young boy kept next to a portrait of his present self. You had emerged unscathed from my dreams and seeing you again I did not have to strip you of a cloak of fantastical perfections.

I was musing on all of this, curled up in my bed, watching the glow from the night-light tremble on the blue roses of the carpet, as I waited for the sleep that would not come; towards morning it came down over my eyes, mixed with disjointed dreams and vague harmonies.

Some weeks later, we received an invitation to attend a grand ball given by the duchess de C... A girl's first ball is an important affair. The whole thing became even more interesting for me, since it was extremely likely you would be at the party, the duchess being one of your best female friends. Balls are our battleground and they are either lost or won. It is where a young lady, having left the shadows of the girls' boarding-school, shines in all her glory. During this short space of time, tradition allows the pretext of a dance to give her a sort of relative freedom and for her the ball is a foyer at the Opéra, where the faces behind the dominoes are exposed. An invitation to dance a quadrille or a mazurka allows her to approach a man and address a few words to him during the moves of the contra-dance. Very often, however, the little book in which she notes down the invitations made to her is full of a long list of names but does not contain the very one she would have wanted.

I had to take care with my outfit; dressing up for a ball is a veritable poem and for a girl, it presents real problems. It must be simple but its simplicity must be rich, two qualities that are mutually exclusive. A flimsy dress all in white, would not, as the ballad says, be quite the right thing. After much dithering I decided on a double-skirted dress of silver lamé chiffon decorated with bunches of forget-me-nots, the colour of which went marvellously with the turquoise jewellery my father had picked out for me at Janisset's. My hair was decorated with turquoise pins, echoing the flowers sewn into my dress. Thus attired, I believed myself capable of appearing amid the magnificent outfits and the famous beauties, without being at too much of a disadvantage. For a simple country girl, I really was quite presentable.

The duchess de C... lived in one of those huge mansions in the district of Saint-Germain, which were built for the grandiose lifestyles of yesteryear and which the modern-day way of life finds it hard to fill. There needs to be a crowd of people and the luxury of a party for it to regain its former animation. From the outside, one would never have guessed the size of this almost princely mansion. All that could be seen from the street was a high wall, squeezed between two houses, framing a monumental carriage entrance; its lintel supported a tablet of green marble with Hôtel de C... in gold letters. A long avenue of century-old lime-trees, stripped of their leaves by winter and shaped into arches in the old French style, led to a huge courtyard at the far end of which stood the mansion. It was pure Louis XIV, with its tall win-

dows, its half-inset pilasters and its Mansart-style roof truss-
ing, that harked back to the architecture of Versailles. A
canopy in pink and white twill, supported by carved wooden
poles, hung out beyond the sumptuously carpeted front steps.
I had time enough to examine all these details in the light
emanating from the cone-shaped Chinese lanterns because,
though the throng of people was select, it was so extensive
that we had to queue as though it were a court reception.
The carriage put us down at the front steps and we threw
our furs over our valet's arm. An enormous Swiss, typically
thickset, stood next to double glass doors, opening and clos-
ing them. In the vestibule, we passed through a hedgerow of
servants wearing their smartest uniforms, powdered white: all
of them tall and motionless and perfectly serious. They were
like the caryatids of domestic staff. They seemed to feel hon-
oured to be servants in such a house. The whole staircase was
lined with immense camellias and was easily big enough to
hold one of today's mini-palaces. On every landing there was
a big mirror, giving the women the opportunity to adjust
their ball outfits on their way up the stairs. Even the lightest
coat ruffles an outfit, and the resultant disarray was betrayed
by the bright light from a chandelier, hanging down on a
golden cable from a domed ceiling where, amid the azure sky
and the clouds, the brush of some pupil of Lebrun or Mig-
nard had used foreshortening to bring to life a mythological
allegory, in line with contemporary taste.

Rectangular landscapes could be seen in the consoles between the windows. Their style was severe, their colour darkened and one might well have attributed them to Poussin or
at least to Gaspard Dughet. This was the opinion of a famous
painter who was climbing the stairs alongside us and who
had put his monocle to his eye to see them better. At the
points where the marvellous wrought iron balustrade turned,
stood marble statues by Lepautre and Théodonon on the
plinths where the handrail was fixed. These held candelabras
whose light reinforced the effect of the chandelier and created a cheerful brightness that meant the party began as soon
as people reached the staircase.

The door to the ante-room was made of old oak and was hung with Gobelin tapestries which were copies of cartoons by Oudry. Beside it stood an usher, dressed in black with a silver chain around his neck, who announced the names of the new arrivals to those in the main drawing room in a voice which resounded to varying degrees depending on the importance of the name.

The duke was tall and thin and, like a thoroughbred greyhound, made up purely of elongated lines. He had an air of perfect nobility and despite his age, he had retained vestiges of his former elegance. No one in the street would have doubted his status. Positioned a few steps from the entrance, he greeted guests with an amiable word, a handshake, a bow, a nod of the head or a smile. He had an exquisite sense of what was appropriate for each individual and was so perfectly gracious that everyone was satisfied and believed themselves the object of special favouritism. He greeted my mother in a friendly and respectful way and, as it was the first time he had seen me, he paid me a brief compliment that was half paternal, half gallant and revealed his old wooing ways.

Near the fireplace stood the duchess. Her make-up showed a total lack of concern for illusion. She was quite clearly wearing a wig and displaying across her daringly exposed flat chest a set of antique diamonds. It was as though she was consumed by her own spirit. Beneath her large swarthy eyelids, her eyes still sparkled with an extraordinary fire. The duchess was dressed in a dark garnet-coloured velvet dress with great flounces and English stitching, and a string of diamonds on the bodice. With a careless hand, she directed a few waves of fresh air at her face from time to time, by means of a large fan, painted by Watteau; and all the while she talked to the groups of people come to pay their respects. She had an extremely grand air about her as she carried out this operation. She exchanged a few remarks with my mother, who introduced me to her, and as I bowed, she brushed my forehead with her cold lips, saying the words: 'Go on, my pretty, and above all, don't you miss out on a single contra-dance.'

Once this ceremony was over, we went into the adjoining drawing room, from which we emerged into the ballroom. Family portraits within magnificent frames, contemporary with the paintings they contained, stood out against red damask walls. These had not been put there out of a sense of noble pride, but merely because they were masterpieces of art. There were works by Clouet, Porbus, Van Dyck, Philippe de Champagne, Largillière, all of which were worthy of an art gallery. What I found pleasing about the luxury of this house was that nothing seemed to have been recently acquired. The paintings, the gold, the damask and the brocard, without being faded, were muted and did not trouble the eyes with the garish brightness of newness. One could sense that this richness was age-old and had always been so. It is rare to come across a ballroom of this size other than in a palace. Numerous candelabras and torchères placed in the bays between the windows, had the effect, with their thousands of candles, of setting the place ablaze with light. And it was as though the azure blue paintings on the ceiling, with their intertwining garlands of nymphs and cupids, were emerging out of a rose-coloured mist. Despite this multitude of flaming light, the room was so vast that there was no shortage of air and it was easy to breathe. The orchestra was up on a kind of platform at the far end of the drawing room in the middle of a clump of rare plants. Velvet bench seats were arranged as in an amphitheatre and on them sat rows and tiers of women whose finery was dazzling even if their beauty was not, though many of them were very pretty. It was a magnificent sight. We had arrived just at the interval between one dance and the next. I sat next to my mother on the end of a bench which had been vacant. This was a new spectacle for me and I watched it with curiosity and amazement. After the men had taken their dancing partners back to their seats, they strolled around the middle of the drawing room, peering to right and left, making a kind of inspection of the women in order to make their choice. This part of the ball was for the young people, and those men who had begun to make their mark on the world ceased to indulge in dancing. There were young embassy attachés, diplomats, prospective auditors at the Council of State, fresh-faced youths who would one day be masters of appeals, army officers on their first campaign, members of the Moutard Club in all their diplomatic seriousness, budding sportsmen with their equestrian dreams, elegant young men whose fin-shaped sideboards were little more than a growth of downy hair, and sons of families who had the precocious confidence that comes of possessing a famous name and a sizeable fortune. Mixed in with these young people, there were even a few serious characters laden with medals, their polished heads shining like ivory under the light of the chandelier or hiding under a wig that was too dark or too fair. As they passed, they addressed a few polite words to the dowagers who had been their contemporaries since childhood. Then they turned away and, now armed with pince-nez, they examined the harem of women laid out before their eyes like highly proficient and disinterested connoisseurs. The first sounds from the orchestra made them rush as fast as their gouty feet could carry them towards the calmer drawing rooms, where bouillotte and écarté were being played at tables lit by candlesticks topped with green shades.

As you might imagine, I wasn't short of invitations. A young Hungarian, in aristocratic dress, covered with braid and embroidery and studded with buttons made of precious stones, bowed gracefully before me and asked me to dance a mazurka. He had regular features and his face was romantically pale, with big dark eyes that were a little wild and a moustache that tapered like a needle. A twenty-two or twenty-three-year-old Englishman who looked like Lord Byron, except that he did not have a limp, came to sign their names in my book, as did an attaché at one of the courts in the North, and several others. Although the old dancing master from the convent boasted that I was one of his best pupils and praised my grace, my suppleness and my sense of time, I was not, I must confess, totally at ease. I was feeling the kind of emotion which, as the newspapers say, is inseparable from a first night. It seemed to me, as timid people tend to imagine, that all eyes were fixed on me. Thankfully my Hungarian friend was an excellent dancer; he supported my first few steps and soon I felt uplifted by the music, drunk with movement and my confidence grew: I allowed myself to be carried along on this whirlwind of floating skirts with a kind of nervous pleasure. But I could not forget what was constantly on my mind, the purpose of my coming to the ball. As I passed near to doors, I glanced quickly into neighbouring drawing rooms, trying to see if you were there. I spotted you at last in a doorway. You were chatting to someone with a brown face, a long nose, a big black beard, wearing a Nizam uniform, a red fez and the order of Medjidieh; he must have been some bey or pasha or other. When the course of the dance brought me back to the front, you were still there, talking animatedly to this Turk with his eastern calm, and you never deigned to cast a glance at the pretty faces flushed from dancing, as they passed before you in a twinkle of light.

I did not lose all hope, however, and for the time being I was quite satisfied knowing you were there. Besides, the evening was not yet over, and some happy coincidence might bring us together. My dancing partner took me back to my place and the men began once more to circulate in the space enclosed by the benches. You took a few steps with your Turkish friend amid this shifting crowd, looking at the women and the outfits, but with the same eyes you would have used to study pictures or statues. From time to time, you would communicate your thoughts to your friend, the pasha, who would smile gravely from inside his beard. I could see all of this from in between the spines of my fan, which I must confess I closed up when you came over to the spot where we were sitting. My heart was beating hard and I felt myself blushing right down to my shoulders. This time it was impossible for me to escape your examination, for you were sticking as closely to the benches as the sparkling fringe of chiffon, lace and flounces, spilling over into the gangway, would allow; but as luck would have it, two or three men friends of my mother's stopped in front of us to pay their respects to

113

her and to some extent to me. This shield of black clothing masked me completely. You had to skirt around the group and I remained unnoticed, despite having inclined my head a little in the hope that you might see me. You could not guess that those tail coats that bowed respectfully hid you from quite a pretty young girl whose only thoughts were of you and who had only come to that ball because of you. I saw you leave the ballroom at the far end, the Turk's red cap acting as a point of reference for me, and helping me not to lose you in this bustle of dark clothing which people wear at parties and funerals alike. All my feelings of joy disappeared and I felt profoundly discouraged. Destiny seemed to enjoy mocking me by keeping you from me. I went through with the dances I had promised and, claiming that I was a little tired, accepted no more invitations. The ball had lost its charm; the outfits seemed faded and the lights were dimming. My father, who was gambling in an adjoining room and had lost about one hundred louis to an old general, came to take us on a tour of the suites and show us the conservatory which was attached to the last room and which everybody said was marvellous. And indeed nothing could have been more sumptuous. It was like being in a virgin forest; there was such a spread of banana trees, grapefruits, palm trees and tropical plants thriving in this warm atmosphere heavy with exotic perfumes. At the far end of the conservatory, a white marble nymph was pouring the contents of her urn into an enormous shell from the South Seas, surrounded by moss and water plants. And there I spotted you once more. Your sister was walking along on your arm but you were in front of us and there was no way we could meet, for we were going in the same direction along the narrow, sandy yellow path, bordered with greenery that wove its way around the clumps of shrubs, flowers and plants.

We went around the rooms a few more times; people were circulating more freely now, as the dancers had moved off towards the buffet to regain their strength. The food was being served in elegant profusion in a picture gallery, fitted out in ebony set off with gold, and decorated with paintings by Desportes depicting flowers, fruit and game. The colours were marvellous and time had only served to enrich them. All these vaguely observed details have been faithfully retained in my memory and I can still remember them in this world where life now seems just a shadowy dream. They are connected for me to such acute sensations that I have been forced to come back to earth. I returned home as sad as I had been happy when I had left; but I passed my air of despondency off as a migraine. Dressing up had been pointless since I had only wanted to be beautiful for you. As I swapped my outfit for a nightgown, I said to myself with a sigh: 'Why didn't he ask me to dance like that Hungarian and that Englishman and those other gentlemen whom I didn't care for in the slightest. It was so simple. What could be more natural at a ball? And yet everyone paid me attention except the one individual whose attention I longed for. There is no hope for my poor love.' I went to bed and a few tears rolled off my eyelashes and on to the pillow...

And that is where Spirite's first dictation ended. The lamp had gone out a long while before, having run out of oil and, like sleepwalkers who have no need of exterior illumination, Malivert had continued to write. Guy wrote page upon page without even realising. Then suddenly the impulse which was guiding his hand ceased and his own thoughts, which had been suspended by those of Spirite, returned to him. The first light of day was filtering through the bedroom curtains. He drew them back and the pale glow of a winter morning showed him there were several sheets of paper on the table, covered with quick fevered writing. And this was his night's work. Though he had written them with his own hand, he knew nothing of their content. With burning curiosity and profound emotion he read the naive and chaste secrets of this charming soul. Needless to say, he had been the unwitting executioner of this adorable creature. Her tardy avowal of love, that came from the other world and was uttered with a sigh by a ghost, threw him into a state of despairing regret and powerless rage against himself. How could he have been so stupid and so blind as to pass up his opportunity for happiness without even noticing it? In the end, though, he calmed down and when he chanced to raise his eyes towards the Venetian mirror he saw Spirite's reflection smiling at him.

CHAPTER 10

It is a strange sensation to learn retrospectively that happiness has passed you by unnoticed, or that you missed your chance and it was your own fault. The sense of regret for the irretrievable is never more bitter: you want to relive days gone by; you make wonderful plans of action; you endow yourself, after the event, with astonishing perspicacity. But life cannot be turned over like an hourglass. The grains that have fallen can never rise back up. Guy de Malivert blamed himself in vain for having been unable to divine this charming creature's feelings. She had not been tucked away in a harem in Constantinople or hidden behind the gates of a convent in Italy or Spain, or watched over by a jealous tutor like Rosina. She had been in his world; he could have seen her every day and there had been no serious barrier to separate them. She loved him; had he asked for her, he would have had her, and he would have enjoyed that rare and supreme bliss of being united on this earth with the soul that was made for his soul. Given the way he adored the ghost, he realised how passionately he would have felt about the woman. Before long, however, his thoughts took another course. He stopped reproaching himself and criticised his mundane grievances. What had he lost? Spirite had conserved her love beyond the grave and was wrenching herself away from the depths of infinity to come down to the sphere in which he lived. Was the passion he was feeling not more noble, more poetic and more ethereal? Was it not closer to eternal love and free therefore of all the earth's eventualities, given that its object was a figure of beauty idealised by death? Even the most perfect human union surely grows weary, sated and tiresome. After a few years, even the most bewitched admirer sees those adored charms pale. The soul becomes less visible through the withered flesh and love looks around in astonishment for its vanished idol.

These reflections, together with the commitments and hum-drum of life that even the most enthusiastic dreamers cannot shirk, took Malivert through to the evening, for which he waited impatiently. Once he had locked himself away in his study, and was sitting near the table as he had done the night before, poised ready to write, the little white hand, slender and blue-veined, reappeared, and indicated to Malivert that he should pick up the pen. He obeyed and his fingers began to move by themselves, without his brain giving them any instruction. His thoughts had been replaced by those of Spirite.

Spirite's Dictation

I wouldn't want to bore you posthumously with tales of all my disappointments. One day, however, I experienced a truly intense feeling of joy and I began to believe that the malicious destiny that seemed to be making a game of concealing me from you was going to stop its teasing. We were to dine the following Saturday at the home of Monsieur de L... This fact would have been of total indifference to me if, during the week, I hadn't found out from the baron de Féroë, who sometimes came to our house, that you were to attend this semi-social, semi-literary feast. Monsieur de L... liked playing host to artists and writers. He was a man of taste, a connoisseur of books and paintings and he had a library and a room where he displayed a flawless selection of pictures. You used sometimes to go to his parties, along with a number of famous authors and other people who were in the process of making a name for themselves. Monsieur de L... prided himself on his ability to discover talent and he was not one of those men who only believe in established reputations. In my intense childish excitement, I said to myself: 'At last I've got him. He's such an elusive character, such a fugitive, but this time he won't get away. When we're sitting at the same table, perhaps next to one another, with the room illuminated by fifty candles, no matter how inattentive he might be, he is bound to notice me... at least, as long as there isn't a basket of flowers or a piece of ornamental china to hide me from him.'

The days still separating me from that happy Saturday, seemed immeasurably long, just as long as lessons at the convent. At last they were over and the three of us, my father, my mother and I, arrived at the home of Monsieur de L..., about half an hour before the meal was due to begin. The guests were scattered around the drawing room; chatting in groups, wandering around, looking at the pictures, opening pamphlets that had been strewn across the table, or passing on the theatre news to a few women sitting on a divan beside the mistress of the house. Among these people were two or three illustrious writers whose names my father told me and whose faces did not seem to me to fit the character of their work. You had not yet arrived, but everyone else was already there, and Monsieur de L... was starting to complain about your lack of punctuality when a tall servant came in carrying a silver tray. On it was a pencil to sign and note the time of the telegram you had sent from Chantilly, containing these words in an electrically charged style: 'Missed the train. Don't wait for me. Terribly sorry.'

It was a cruel disappointment. All week I had entertained a hope that was now vanishing just as it should have been fulfilled. I was gripped by a feeling of sadness which I had extreme difficulty disguising, and my cheeks, made rosy by the excitement, drained of colour. Thankfully, the doors to the dining room opened and the butler announced 'dinner is served'. The movement amongst the guests prevented anyone from seeing my distress. When everyone was seated, a place remained empty on my left. It was your seat, and so that I could be in no doubt about it, your name was written in a beautiful round-hand on a card, decorated with delicate, coloured arabesques, placed next to your row of glasses. The irony of fate was thus complete. Without that tedious problem with the railway, I would have had you brushing against my dress for the whole duration of the meal, your hand perhaps touching mine in the course of the thousand little services which even the least attentive gallantry deems it necessary that a man carry out for a woman. At first, as with every prelude to conversation, a few banal words would have been exchanged between us; then, once the ice was broken, the discussion would have become more intimate and before long, your spirit would have understood my heart. Perhaps you wouldn't have disliked me, and although you'd just arrived back from Spain, perhaps you'd have forgiven the rosy whiteness of my complexion and the pale gold of my hair. If you'd come to that dinner, your life and mine would undoubtedly have taken a different turn. You would no longer be a bachelor, I would be alive, and I wouldn't be reduced to making declarations to you from beyond the grave. The love with which you have been smitten for my ghost leads me to believe, without being too conceited, that you wouldn't have been insensitive to my earthly charms; but that was not to be. That unoccupied seat, which isolated me from the other guests, seemed to be a symbol of my fate. For me it represented the hopelessness of my waiting, and my solitude amid a mass of people. That sinister omen proved all too accurate. My neighbour on my left side was, as I have since learnt, an extremely amiable, though wise academic. He tried several times to get me to speak but I only replied in monosyllables and those monosyllables were so inappropriate to the man's questions that he became disheartened, assumed I was a fool and abandoned me in order to converse with the woman sitting on the other side of him.

Some of the dishes barely touched my lips. My heart felt so heavy I couldn't eat. The dinner finally came to an end and everyone moved into the drawing room; a variety of conversations started up, according to the guests' common interests. In a group close enough to the armchair where I was sitting for me to be able to hear all that was being said, your name, pronounced by Monsieur d'Aversac, excited my curiosity. 'That devil Malivert,' said d'Aversac, 'is besotted by his pasha. And as for the pasha, he is mad about Malivert; they're never apart nowadays. Mohamed or Mustapha, I'm not too sure of his name, wants to take Guy off to Egypt. He's talking about putting a steamer at his disposal, so they could get as far as the first waterfalls; but Guy, being as barbaric as the Turk is civilised, would prefer a small sailing boat, thinking that more quaint. The plan appeals to Malivert. He finds it awfully cold in Paris and he'd love to spend the winter in Cairo, continuing the study of Arab architecture he began at the Alhambra. But if he does go out there, I fear we'll never see him again. He'll embrace Islam like Hassan, the hero of *Namouna*.'

'He's quite capable of doing that,' replied a young man who had joined the group. 'He has always shown an indifference for Western civilisation.'

'Rubbish,' responded another man. 'Once he's put on a few authentic outfits, taken a dozen or so steam baths, bought a slave or two from the Djellabs and then resold them at a loss; once he's climbed the pyramids and sketched the pug-nosed profile of the sphinx, then he'll be back to tread the asphalt of the Boulevard des Italiens in peace. This is after all the only habitable place in the universe.'

This conversation threw me into a state of extreme agitation. You would be going away. For how long? Who knew? Would I get the chance to meet you before you left and at least give you an image of me to take with you? It was a blissful idea that I no longer dared believe in, after so much fruitless effort.

When I got home, I first reassured my mother who had thought me ill because of my paleness and had no suspicion of what was going on in my soul. Then I set about some deep reflection on my position. I wondered if this stubbornness of circumstance to keep us apart wasn't some sort of private piece of advice proffered by fate, which it would be dangerous not to heed. Perhaps you would turn out to be the death of me. Perhaps I was wrong to be so obstinate about crossing your path. This was only my mind talking, for my heart would not accept the idea; it wanted to run the risks of the love it felt to the last. I felt unassailably attached to you, and this link, so frail in appearance, was sturdier than a chain of diamonds. Sadly, it only bound *me*. 'The lot of women is such a harrowing one,' I told myself, 'condemned to waiting, inaction and silence. They cannot show their preferences without losing all semblance of propriety. They must endure the love they inspire and they must never declare the love they feel. From the moment my soul was awakened, it has been prey to a unique feeling that is pure, absolute and eternal, and the human being that is the object of that feeling might never know anything about it. How can I make him aware that a girl, whom he would surely love if he could suspect such a secret, lives and breathes only for him?'

For a moment I had the idea of writing you one of those letters which they say authors sometimes get. Beneath a veil of admiration, they allow another kind of sentiment to be divined. They request a rendezvous at the theatre or they propose a walk - something that wouldn't be compromising. But my feminine refinement was appalled by such a means, and I feared you might take me for a bluestocking seeking your patronage in order to get a novel into the *Revue des Deux Mondes*.

D'Aversac had been right. The following week you left for Cairo with your pasha friend. Your departure put off my hopes indefinitely and inspired in me a sense of melancholy which I found hard to hide. My reason for living had ceased. I no longer had any interest in my appearance and when I moved in society circles, I let my maid decide on my outfit. What point was there in being beautiful? You weren't there. I was still beautiful enough, though, to be surrounded like Penelope by a court of suitors. Little by little, our drawing room, which was frequented by my father's friends – serious somewhat mature men – came to be populated on our Friday evenings by younger, very attentive individuals. Dashing young men stood in doorways; they had smart curly hair, and had thought long and hard about the knots of their ties. I could see them surreptitiously throwing passionate, fascinated glances towards me. Others sighed whenever there was a flourish on the piano during the steps of the contra-dance. This didn't affect me in the slightest and I put it down to shortness of breath. A few more daring ones risked some moral and poetic remarks on the blissful nature of a well-matched marriage and claimed they were especially made for such lawful bliss. How well groomed they all were, how faultless and impeccable and perfectly refined. The hair cologne came from Houbigant's; their clothes were tailored by Renard. What more could an exacting and romantic imagination ask for? So these handsome young people seemed naively surprised that they didn't make much of an impression on me. The more vexed amongst them went as far as to suspect me of being poetical. A few serious admirers put themselves forward. My parents were asked for my hand on more than one occasion; but when I was consulted, I always replied in the negative, and came up with excellent reasons just at the right moment. They didn't press me. I was so young that there was no cause for me to rush into something, then regret the haste of the choice later. My mother thought I was hiding my preference and questioned me; I was about to open up to her but an overwhelming sense of propriety held me back. This love, which only *I* was feeling, and which you were unaware of, seemed to me a secret that I shouldn't divulge without your consent. It didn't wholly belong to me; half of it was yours; and so I kept quiet. Besides, how could I confess, even to the most indulgent of mothers, what might easily have appeared to be a mad passion, based as it was on a childhood impression, conceived in the visiting room at a convent, and persistently harboured in the depths of my soul? Nothing could justify it on a human level. I couldn't be blamed for my choice; nor was it an impossible one. And if I had talked to my mother, I'm sure she would have tried to bring us together, and found a cunning way to make you speak to me. On such occasions the most honest and virtuous women know how such things can be done. But this idea disgusted my propriety as a virgin. I wanted no intermediary to come between you and me. You had to notice me and divine my secret yourself. This was the price I had to pay in order to be happy and forgive myself for having been the first woman to love you. My girlish sense of propriety needed this solace and this excuse. It was neither pride nor a concern with my appearance, but a pure sentiment of feminine dignity.

Time passed and you returned from Egypt. People started

talking about your attentiveness to Madame d'Ymbercourt and saying you were madly in love with her. Fear clutched my heart. I wanted to see my rival. She was pointed out to me in her box at the Italiens. I tried to judge her impartially. I thought she was beautiful but lacking in charm and finesse, like a copy of a classical statue done by a second-rate sculptor. She brought together everything that makes up a fool's idea of the perfect woman and I was astonished that you were in the least attracted to this idol. Madame d'Ymbercourt's face, which at first sight looked so regular, lacked any unusual features, natural grace or unexpected charm. That is how she looked that evening, and that is how she would always be. Despite what people said, I felt proud that I wasn't jealous of this woman. The rumours circulating about your marriage were, however, gaining strength. As bad news always reaches those it concerns, I was aware of everything that was happening between you and Madame d'Ymbercourt. One rumour said the first wedding banns had been made public; another went as far as to fix the precise date of the ceremony. I didn't have any way of ascertaining whether these rumours were true or false. Since everyone had the impression the matter was settled and that it was quite acceptable in every respect, I really had no option but to believe it. Yet the secret voice of my heart told me you didn't love Madame d'Ymbercourt. People often engage in loveless marriage, though: to get a house, to normalise their position in society or because they feel the need to rest after the misdemeanours and hotheadedness of youth. A profound feeling of despair came over me. I saw my life coming to a close and the chaste dream I had cherished for so long vanishing for ever. I could no longer even think of you in the most mysterious recess of my soul; for you belonged to another in the eyes of God and men alike; and those thoughts, which up until then had been innocent, now became guilty. Yet nothing had slipped into my girlish passion that could have made my guardian angel blush. Once, I came across you in the Bois de Boulogne. You were on horseback riding alongside Madame d'Ymbercourt's barouche. But I threw myself down on to the floor of my carriage, taking as much care to hide from you now as I would once have taken to be seen by you. This brief glimpse was the last I saw of you.

I was barely seventeen. What would become of me? How could I live out a life that had been secretly wrecked at its outset? Would I have to accept one of those individuals of whom my parents, in their wisdom, would approve? That is what many girls have done in similar circumstances when, like me, they were separated from their ideal partner by some obscure twist of fate. My sense of loyalty would not allow such a compromise, however. To my mind, my first and only thoughts of love had been for you, and on this earth I could only belong to you. Any other union would have seemed a kind of adultery. My heart had just one page; you had unwittingly written your name on it and no other should take its place. Your marriage would not make me any less faithful. You were unaware of my love and so you were free whilst I was bound. The idea of being another man's wife I found unbearably dreadful and, after refusing several admirers and knowing how difficult it is for an old spinster to live in the world, I resolved to leave secular society and devote myself to religion. Only God could shelter my grief and perhaps bring me consolation.

CHAPTER 11

I entered the convent of the Sisters of Mercy as a novice, despite my parents' protests and pleading. They tempered my courage but could not shake it. However firm the resolution with which one is armed, it is awful when the time comes to separate for good. At the far end of a long corridor, a gate marks the boundary between the world and the cloister. The family can accompany the virgin who is devoting herself to God as far as that threshold, but no member of secular society may cross it. Sullen, veiled faces wait impassively for an end to the last embraces, and then the gate opens just enough to allow the novice to pass. The arms of a ghost seem to carry her away and the gate slams shut again with a clatter of iron, which is prolonged in the silence of the corridors like a rumble of thunder. The sound of a coffin lid shutting is no more doom-laden and resounds no more painfully on the heart. I could feel myself going pale and an icy coldness enveloped me. I had just taken my first step outside life on earth which, from that moment on, would be closed off from me. I went deep into that cold space where passions are extinguished, memories are erased and the murmurings of secular society cannot reach. Nothing there exists except the thought of God. And that is enough to fill the frightening void and the silence as profound as that of the grave that reigns in such places. I can speak about this now because I am dead.

My piety, though tender and fervent, did not stretch to mystic exaltation. It was a human motive rather than an imperious calling that had made me seek peace in the shadows of the cloister. I was the victim of a shipwrecked soul which had foundered on an unknown reef, and my drama, invisible to everyone, had come to its tragic conclusion. Initially, I experienced what is known in a life of religious devotion as periods of barrenness and fatigue. I turned back towards the world; I had vague feelings of despair; all of which were the last attempts of the spirit of secular society wanting to reclaim its hunting ground. Soon, however, this tumult calmed. The habit of prayer and religious rites, the regularity of the services and the monotony of the rules, that were calculated to overcome the rebellion of body and soul, turned a mind, still with too many memories of earth, towards heaven. Your image lived on in my heart but I managed to love you just through God.

The convent of the Sisters of Mercy is not one of those romantic cloisters, which people on earth would imagine could shelter a despairing love. There were no pointed arches, no little columns festooned with ivy, no moonbeams shining through the trefoil of a broken rose window to throw their light on to a tombstone inscription. There was no chapel with stained glass windows and slender pillars and keystones with openwork tracery - an excellent decorative or dioramic motif. Religiousness that seeks to uphold Christianity through its quaint, poetic aspects would have found no subject on which to base descriptions reminiscent of Chateaubriand. The construction is modern and so there are absolutely no dark recesses in which to set a legend. There is nothing to entertain the eyes; no ornamentation, no artistic fantasy, no painting, no sculpture; just hard dry lines. A white light like the light of a winter's day illuminates the paleness of the long corridors, whose walls are interrupted by the symmetrical doors of the cells. It makes the shiny floors icy cold with its oblique light skimming over them. Everywhere there is a pervading sullen severity that is heedless of beauty and wouldn't dream of clothing a concept with a form. This sombre architecture has the advantage of not distracting souls which must lose themselves in God. In the high windows there is a tight criss-cross of iron bars and their dark grid pattern only allows a glimpse of the blue or grey sky outside. Living there, you are in the middle of a fortress raised against the pitfalls of the world. The cloister's sturdiness is sufficient. Beauty would be superfluous.

The chapel itself is only half given over to worship by

committed Christians from the outside world. A large gate decorated with thick green curtains stretches from the ground up to the vaulted ceiling. Like the portcullis of a fortified town, it separates the church from the chancel that is reserved for the nuns. Adorning each side are wooden stalls with plain engraving that have been rubbed so much they shine. At the back, towards the centre, are three seats for the mother superior and her two assistants. That is where the sisters go to hear the divine office, with their veils lowered and their long black robes trailing behind them. On the robes are wide bands of white material like the cross on a funeral drape, with its arms cut off. From the lattice-work gallery where the novices stand, I used to watch them cross themselves before the mother superior and the altar, then kneel down, prostrate themselves and sink into their stalls which had now become prie-dieux. At the elevation of the host, the central curtain is half opened and this allows you a glimpse of the priest consummating the Holy Sacrifice at the altar opposite the chancel. The fervour of this adoration edified me and gave strength to my resolution to break away from the world, into which it was still possible for me to return. Amid the atmosphere of rapture and incense, with the trembling candle-light casting a pale beam over those prostrate brows, my soul felt it was sprouting wings and tending increasingly to rise up towards ethereal places. The chapel ceiling was filled with blue and gold, and in a gap in the sky I seemed to be able to see the angels reaching towards me with a smile from the edge of a sunlit cloud. They gestured to me to go with them and I no longer noticed the false colour of the distemper, the dubious taste of the chandelier or the poorness of the paintings in their dark wooden frames.

The time had almost come for me to take my vows. All around me there was flattery and encouragement, subtle warnings, mystical cajoling, hopes for perfect blissful happiness: the kind of things people lavish on young novices in convents when they are about to consummate their sacrifice and devote themselves for ever to the Lord. I didn't need this support. I could walk up to the altar with confidence. As I was forced, or so I thought, to give you up, I missed nothing of the world, except my parents' tenderness. And my determination not to go back to it was unshakeable.

When my tests were over, the solemn day came. The convent, which was normally so peaceful, was enlivened by a kind of excitement that was contained by the strict discipline of the convent. The nuns were coming and going along the corridors, forgetting sometimes the ghostly walk which the rules advised; the donning of a habit is after all a great occasion. A new sheep is joining the flock and the whole of the fold rejoices. The society garb in which the novice is dressed for the last time is the subject of curiosity, joy and amazement. That satin and lace, those pearls and gems, all of them intended to represent the pomp and vanity of Satan, are regarded with a kind of fearful admiration. Wearing this finery, I was led to the chancel. The mother superior and her assistants were in their places, and in their stalls the nuns were hunched in prayer. I uttered those sacramental words which would separate me for ever from the land of the living, and as the ritual of the ceremony demands, I used my foot to push aside the plush square of velvet which, at certain points, I'd had to kneel down on. I pulled off my necklace and my bracelets and got rid of my finery as a sign of my renunciation of vanity and luxury. I gave up the interest a woman has in her appearance. It wasn't hard for me, since I wasn't allowed to make you happy or be beautiful for you.

Then came the most feared and miserable scene of this religious drama; the time when they cut the new nun's hair, which from that time forward would be a needless conceit. It makes you look like a condemned prisoner, except that this victim is innocent or at the very least she has been purified by repentance. Although I had sacrificed quite sincerely, and from the bottom of my heart, all human attachment, a deathly paleness came over my face when the blade of the scissors sliced into my head of long fair hair, as it was held up by a nun. The golden curls fell in thick clumps on to the flagstones of the sacristy where I had been taken. I stared as they rained down around me. I was shattered and gripped by a secret horror. The coldness of the metal as it brushed the back of my neck made me shiver nervously, as an axe would. My teeth chattered. The prayer I was trying to say never reached my lips. An icy sweat like the sweat of death pangs soaked my temples. My eyesight was giving me difficulty and the lamp hanging in front of the altar to the Virgin seemed to vanish into a fog. My knees gave way beneath me, and as I stretched out my arms to grasp hold of the void, I only had time to say 'I'm dying'.

They gave me smelling salts and when I came round I was as amazed by the brightness of the day as a ghost that leaves its grave. I found myself in the arms of the sisters, and they supported me with calm attentiveness as though they were used to such fainting fits.

'It's nothing,' the youngest of the sisters told me sympathetically. 'The most difficult part is over. Just commend yourself to the Blessed Virgin and everything will be fine. The same thing happened to me when I took my vows. It's a last attempt by the Devil.'

Two sisters dressed me in the black habit of the order and put a white stole around me. Then, taking me back to the chancel, they laid the veil over my head. This symbolic shroud made me dead to the world and left me visible only to God. I'd heard of a pious legend, which said that if you asked heaven for mercy from behind the folds of the funeral veil, then it would be granted. Once the veil was around me, I implored divine goodness to indulge me by revealing my love to you after my death, if such a wish were not reprehensible in any way. It seemed my prayer had been answered for I experienced a sudden sense of inner joy and great relief. This had been my secret sorrow, the needle pricking my heart, making me suffer night and day like a hair shirt hidden beneath my clothes. I had quite given you up in this world but my soul could not agree to keep its secret eternally.

Shall I tell you of my existence at the convent? Day after day is rigidly the same. Every hour there is a prayer, an act of devotion, or a task that must be carried out. Life marches steadily on to eternity, happy to be nearing its goal. And yet this calm façade sometimes conceals a great deal of fatigue, sadness and restlessness. Though your thoughts are quelled by prayer and meditation, they do wander off into reverie. Nostalgia for the world comes over you. You miss freedom, family and nature. You dream about the expansive horizon flooded with light and the meadows studded with flowers; the hills with their undulating wooded slopes and the blueish smoke that rises up from the countryside in the evenings; the road where the carriages roll by and the river that the boats cross; you dream about life and activity and sounds of happiness and the endless variety of things that is continually being refreshed. You want to walk and run and fly. You envy a bird for its wings. You are restless in your tomb. You imagine scaling the high walls of the convent and your mind returns to the places you loved, to the scenes of your childhood and youth that come to life again in magically sharp detail. You construct pointless plans for your happiness, forgetting that you are locked in forever by your irrevocable decision. The most devout souls are exposed to these temptations and memories, to these mirages which willpower rejects and prayer tries to dissipate. But in the silence and solitude of the cell, within those four white walls with just a dark wooden crucifix for decoration, they crop up no less often. Thoughts of you, which were at first dismissed by the fervour of my initial time there, came back to me more frequently and more tenderly. My heart was painfully weighed down with the grief I felt at having lost my chance for blissful happiness, and often silent tears flowed down my pale cheeks without my even realising. Sometimes at night I would cry in my dreams and in the morning I would find my rough bolster completely soaked with this bitter dew. In my happier dreams I saw myself with you on the front steps of a villa, having returned from a walk; I climbed a white staircase covered with jagged blueish patches of shadow cast by the tall trees nearby. I was your wife and you glanced at me tenderly and protectively. All barriers between us had disappeared. My soul could not accept such cheerful deception and fought against it as it would have fought against sin. I confessed and did my penitence. I stayed awake all night praying, I battled against sleep so as to escape these guilty fantasies, and yet they always returned.

The struggle was sapping my strength and it wasn't long before my health began to deteriorate. Though I was not sickly, I was delicate. The roughness of life in a cloister, with its fasting, its abstinences, its scourging of the flesh, the tiring night-time prayers, the sepulchral cold of the church, the rigours of a long winter from which I was poorly protected by a thin muslin habit, all these things were having a disastrous effect on my constitution; on top of this there was the battle in my soul, the alternate feelings of exaltation and despondency, of doubt and fervour, and the fear that I could only offer my divine Spouse a heart distracted by a human attachment and that this could engender celestial vengeance, for God is jealous and cannot abide sharing; and perhaps Madame d'Ymbercourt was making me jealous too. My complexion had become lack-lustre like candle wax; my eyes looked larger because of my thinness and they shone feverishly in their bruised sockets; the veins in my temples stood out in a network of dark blue. My lips had lost their fresh pink colouring, leaving the violets of my impending death to start blossoming. My hands had become slender and transparent and as pale as a ghost's hands. Death is not considered at the convent as it is in society; its approach is regarded with joy. It is the release of the soul, the open door to heaven, the end of the tests and the beginning of beatitude. God welcomes His favourites, those He loves, before anyone else and He cuts short their passage through this valley of misery and tears. A funereal chant of hopeful prayer surrounds the deathbed of a dying nun. The last rites cleanse her of any terrestrial stains and the light of the next life already shines on her. For her sisters, she is an object of envy, not of fear.

Unafraid, I watched the fatal day approach. I hoped God would forgive me my one and only love and would be happy to admit me to His grace. That love had been so chaste, so pure, so unintentional, and as soon as I had seen it to be reprehensible, I had striven to forget it. I soon became so weak that I would faint during my prostrations and stay stretched out as though I were dead behind my veil, with my face against the floor. Everyone respected my stillness and assumed I was in rapture. Then, seeing that I wasn't getting up, two nuns leant down towards me, straightened me up like a lifeless body and with their hands underneath my arms, they guided me, or rather carried me, back to my cell, which I was soon to leave no more. I spent hours on end fully clothed on my bed, saying my rosary with the beads between my wasted fingers, lost in some vague meditation, wondering whether my wish would be granted after my death. My strength was visibly waning and though the medicine I was given for my sickness could lessen my suffering, it could not cure me. I didn't want to be cured anyway, for beyond life I had a long-cherished hope and its possible realisation inspired in me a kind of curiosity about things beyond the grave. My passage from this world to the other came about in the gentlest of ways. All mental and material links were broken off, except for one thread a thousand times finer than the gossamer threads that float in the air on the most beautiful autumn days. This alone held back my soul, which was ready to open its wings to the breath of infinity. Alternate light and shade throbbed before my anxious eyes like the intermittent glow a night-light casts before it dies. I did my best to join in mentally with the whispered prayers of the nuns kneeling around me. These only reached me as a confused drone of vague and distant rumblings. My thoughts and my senses, now deadened to everything on earth, had abandoned my brain to flutter hesitantly in a bizarre dream world, between the realms of the material and the immaterial. They no more belonged to one than to the other. And all the while, my pale ivory fingers mechanically crumpled and smoothed out the folds in the sheet. Finally my death pangs began and I was laid out on the ground with a bag of ashes beneath my head so I could die in the humble attitude befitting a poor servant of God returning herself, dust to dust. I became increasingly short of air. I was suffocating. A feeling of extraordinary dread gripped my chest. My natural instinct was battling against destruction. But soon that pointless fight ceased and with a feeble sigh my soul was breathed out through my lips.

CHAPTER 12

Human words cannot describe the sensation of a soul that is freed from its corporeal prison and passes from this life to the other, from time into eternity and from the finite into the infinite. My motionless body, already covered in a dull shade of white and released by death, was lying on the funeral couch surrounded by praying nuns. I was as detached from it as a butterfly can be from a chrysalis – that empty shell, that shapeless skin – which it abandons to spread its young wings in the unknown light to which it has suddenly been exposed. An intermittent period of profound darkness had been followed by a dazzle of brilliance, a broadening of horizons and the disappearance of all boundaries and obstacles, and this intoxicated me with an inexpressible feeling of joy. An explosion of new sensations helped me understand the mysteries that are impenetrable for earthly minds and organs. Freed from the clay that must obey the laws of gravity and that had weighed me down just a short while before, I now set off with fantastic alacrity into the unfathomable realm of the ethereal. Distance no longer existed for me, and my pure desire took me to where I wanted to be. I traced great circles passing swarms of souls and spirits, flying faster than the speed of light through the hazy blue of space, as though I wanted to take hold of this vastness.

A teeming mass of light, shining like diamond dust, made up the atmosphere. Each grain of this sparkling dust, as I soon realised, was a soul. There were currents and swirls and eddies and waves and shimmerings, as one gets in the kind of impalpable powder that is spread over sounding boards to study the vibrations; each of these movements caused a fresh upsurge of brilliance within the magnificent whole. The figures that mathematics might come up with to calculate this would plunge into the depths of infinity but, even with those millions of zeros adding their enormous power to the initial figure, they could not give even an approximate idea of the frightening multitude of souls that made up that light; a light as different from material light as day is different from night.

Alongside those souls that had already been through the tests of life since the creation of our world and other universes, were souls in waiting, virginal souls, there until their turn should come to be made incarnate in a body on a planet of whatever system. There were enough of them to populate for thousands of years all the universes that God breathed out and that He will reabsorb by drawing breath again, when He becomes weary of His work. These souls differed from each other in essence and appearance, depending on the world in which they were to live but, despite the infinite variety of types amongst them, they all resembled the divine type and were made in the image of their creator. The basic element in each of them was a spark from heaven. Some of these souls were as white as diamonds, others were coloured like rubies and emeralds, sapphires and topaz and amethyst. For want of other points of reference that you would understand, I use the names of these stones, these worthless pebbles, these opaque crystals. But they are as dark as ink and the most brilliant examples would only be dots against this backcloth of living splendour.

From time to time some great angel would pass by, carrying an order from God to the ends of infinity and making the universes vibrate with the beating of its huge wings. The Milky Way was a river of molten suns streaming through the sky. I could see the stars in their true shape and grandeur. The human imagination could never conceive of such enormity. They sparkled with immense wild flashes and behind them and in the spaces between them I could make out more of them and others again besides at increasingly breathtaking depths. The end of the firmament was nowhere to be seen and I could easily have thought myself locked inside a huge sphere whose interior was all studded with stars. Their illumination was white and yellow and blue and green and red and it reached such levels of intensity and vividness that the light of our sun seems dark in comparison. And yet the eyes of my soul could tolerate it quite easily. I went here and there, up and down, and in the space of one second I travelled millions of leagues through the light of dawn, through rainbow reflections, gold and silver irradiation, diamond phosphorescence and shooting stars, seeing everything in all its splendour and beauty and rapture through divine light. I could hear the music of the spheres, an echo of which reached Pythagoras's ears, for mysterious numbers, which are the mainsprings of the universe, were marking time. With a harmonious hum, as powerful as thunder and as gentle as a flute, our world was carried along by its central star and turned slowly in space. At just one glance I took in the planets from Mercury to Neptune, as they traced their ellipses alongside their satellites. A sudden feeling of intuition revealed to me the names by which heaven knows them. I understood their structure, their thoughts, their aims. No secret of their wondrous lives was hidden from me. This divine poem had suns for letters and I could read it like an open book. I wish I were allowed to write a few pages explaining everything to you! But you still live in the gloom of a lowlier and darker world, and your eyes would be blinded by this dazzling brightness.

Despite the indescribable beauty of this marvellous spectacle, I still hadn't forgotten earth, that wretched dwelling place I had just left. My love had conquered death and was following me around beyond the grave. To my divine delight and glorious joy I could see that you loved no one, that your soul was free and that it could be mine for ever. I knew then what I had always sensed. We were destined for each other. Our souls formed the kind of heavenly couple that melts together to make an angel; but in order for those two halves of the supreme whole to be reunited in immortality they must have sought each other out in life, seen into each other through the veils of the flesh and overcome tests, obstacles and distractions. Only *I* had felt the presence of my soul mate, and had rushed towards it, driven by an infallible instinct. *Your* perception was more confused and had just put you on your guard against mundane ties and love affairs. You realised that none of these souls was made for you. Beneath a cold exterior you were a passionate man, reserving yourself for a higher ideal. Thanks to the privilege granted me, I was able to make you aware of that love. During my lifetime you had been unaware of it but now I hoped to inspire in you the desire to follow me into the sphere where I live. I had no regrets. What is the happiest human relationship alongside the joy two souls share in the eternal kiss of divine love? Until that supreme moment came, my task was restricted to stopping the world from committing you to its ways and separating you from me for ever. Marriage is binding through this world and the other. But you did not love Madame d'Ymbercourt; my position as a spirit allowed me to read your heart and I had nothing to fear in this respect. You might, however, tire of not seeing the ideal you dreamed of appear, and out of weariness, apathy, despair and the need to put an end to things, you could have fallen into that dull marriage.

Leaving the realms of luminosity behind, I came down to earth. I could see it turning beneath me, surrounded by its hazy atmosphere and its bands of cloud. I found you without difficulty and I joined you as an invisible witness to your life, reading your mind, and influencing it without your knowledge. You never suspected my presence and it enabled me to usher away any ideas, desires or whims which might have diverted you from the goal towards which I was directing you. Little by little I freed your soul from everything that chained it to the earth. To keep a better watch on you I cast a hazy spell over your home to make you love it. You felt it around you like an impalpable mute caress and you experienced an inexplicable feeling of well-being. It seemed to you, although you couldn't know why, that your happiness was locked away within those walls I inhabited. When a lover reads his favourite poet next to a good fire on a stormy night – while his mistress sleeps in the alcove, absorbed in sweet dreams, with her arm draped over her head – he experiences this feeling of intimate, blissful happiness and loving confinement. There is nothing in the outside world which would make it worth his while to cross his beloved threshold. For him, everything is enclosed within this room. Gradually I had to prepare you for my apparition and mysteriously strike up a relationship with you. Communication is difficult between a spirit and an uninitiated living being. A profound gulf separates this world from the other one. I had crossed it but that wasn't enough. I had to make myself perceptible to your eyes, blindfolded as they still were, unable to see through the opaqueness of things into the immaterial world.

Madame d'Ymbercourt was still pursuing her idea of marriage, luring you into her home to stimulate your interest with her attentions. By substituting my will for your dulled mind, I made you write that reply to the lady's note that caused you such surprise. The idea of the supernatural dawned on you and after more careful consideration you realised that a mysterious power was part of your life. The sigh I uttered when, despite my warning, you made up your mind to go out, may have been as feeble and indistinct as a vibrating string on a school harp, but it troubled you profoundly and struck a supernatural chord in your soul. You had perceived in it a tone of feminine suffering. I was still unable to manifest myself to you in a more precise way, as you had not yet freed yourself from the shadows of the material world. So I appeared to the baron de Féroë, a disciple of Swedenborg and a visionary, to recommend that he make that mysterious remark to you which put you on your guard against the perils you were running and gave you the desire to penetrate the world of the spirits to which my love was calling you. You know the rest. Am I to go back up there or stay down here? And will the ghost be happier than the woman?...

At this point the impulse which was making Malivert's pen race over the paper ceased and the young man's thoughts which had been suspended by Spirite's influence took possession of his brain once more. He read what he had just written unconsciously and resolved to love this charming soul that had suffered for him during its brief time on earth, and to do so exclusively until he died. 'But what kind of relationship will we have?' he wondered. 'Will Spirite carry me off to the places where she soars, or will she flit around and be visible only to me? Will she answer me if I speak to her and how will I hear her?'

These were questions which it was not easy to answer; so after debating them, Malivert put them aside and remained immersed in a long reverie until Jack roused him from it by announcing the baron de Féroë.

The two friends shook hands and the Swede with the pale golden moustache threw himself into an armchair.

'Guy,' he said, stretching his feet out on to the fireguard, 'I have come quite simply to ask you for some breakfast. I came out early and as I was passing your house, I fell prey to this whim to pay you a visit; it's almost as early as a bailiff would come round.'

'You did the right thing, baron. What a nice idea!' Malivert replied, as he rang for Jack and gave him orders for breakfast to be served and for two places to be set.

'It looks, my dear Guy, as though you haven't been to bed,' said the baron, looking at the candles that had burnt right down to the sockets and the sheets of writing scattered over the table. You were working last night. Is it out soon? What is it, a novel or a poem?'

'It may be a poem,' replied Malivert, 'but it's not my composition. I merely held the pen for an inspiration that was superior to my own.'

'I understand,' the baron continued. 'Apollo was dictating and Homer was writing. Those are the best kinds of verse.'

'This poem, if that's what it is, is not in verse and it wasn't a mythological god that whispered it to me.'

'I'm sorry, I was forgetting, you're a romantic. As far as you're concerned, Apollo and the Muses should be left in Chompré's dictionary or *Letters to Emily*.'

'Since you, my dear baron, have in some ways been my occult priest and introduced me to the supernatural, there is no reason for me to hide from you the fact that these sheets which you took to be a piece of *copy,* as printers say, were dictated to me last night and on previous nights by the spirit

140

that has taken an interest in me and that seems to have known you on earth, for your name crops up in her tale.'

'You've been making use of a *medium*,' replied the baron de Féroë, 'because the links are not yet properly established between you and the spirit that is paying you visits; but soon you will no longer have any need of these slow, crude methods of communication. Your souls will intertwine through thought and desire without any outward sign.'

Jack came to announce that breakfast was served. Malivert was totally overwhelmed by this strange adventure, a piece of good fortune from beyond the grave that Don Juan would have envied, and he hardly touched the morsels placed before him. The baron de Féroë did eat but with a Swedenborgian abstemiousness, for those who want to live a life of communication with the spirit world must dilute material things as far as possible.

'This is excellent tea you have,' said the baron. 'White-tipped green tea, picked after the first rains of spring; mandarins drink it without sugar, sipping it from cups covered with metal filigree so they won't burn their fingertips. It is the drink *par excellence* of dreamers and the stimulation it produces is entirely intellectual. Nothing stirs the sluggishness of human existence more gently or better predisposes one to see things that the common herd does not. As you will now be living in an immaterial sphere, I recommend this beverage to you. But, my dear Guy, you're not listening to me. And I can understand your distraction. Such a new situation must be strange and worrying for you.'

'Yes,' replied Malivert, 'I admit I'm in a kind of drunken state, and I constantly wonder whether I'm the victim of some hallucination or other.'

'Dismiss such ideas. They would make the spirit flee for ever. Do not try to explain the inexplicable. Abandon yourself with absolute faith and submission to the influence that is guiding you. The slightest doubt would bring about a rupture and cause you eternal regret. It is rare that permission is granted for souls which have not met in life to be united in heaven. Take advantage of it and show that you are worthy of such happiness.'

'I will be worthy of it, believe me, and I won't make Spirite suffer the same pain that in all innocence I inflicted on her when she lived in this world. Now I come to think of it, in the tale she dictated to me, that adorable soul didn't tell me the name she bore on earth.'

'Are you really keen to know? Then go to Père-Lachaise, climb the hill, and near the chapel you will see a white marble gravestone. Upon it there is a sculpted cross, inscribed and decorated at its crosspiece with a wreath of roses and delicate marble leaves, the masterpiece of a well-known sculptor. Within the circle formed by the wreath, a short inscription will tell you what I have not formally been authorised to tell you. The tomb will speak to you in its silent language in my stead, although in my opinion your curiosity is pointless. What does an earthly name matter when eternal love is at stake? You're not yet entirely detached from human ideas, though. That's understandable. It hasn't been long since you stepped outside the circle that encloses ordinary life.'

The baron de Féroë left. Guy dressed, had his horse harnessed and raced around the most renowned florists' in search of a spray of white lilacs. It was the middle of winter and he had difficulty finding what he wanted. But in Paris, the impossible does not exist for anyone who can pay. And so he found what he wanted and climbed the hill with his heart beating and his eyes moist.

A few flakes of snow that had not yet melted sparkled like silver tears on the dark leaves of the yews and the cypresses, the little fir trees and the ivy, and added a white border to the moulding of the gravestones and to the tops and arms of the gravestone crosses. The sky was low, yellow-grey in colour and as heavy as lead, the perfect sky to hang over a cemetery. The bitter North wind moaned as it passed along those alleys of monuments made to fit the dead and measured strictly in relation to the nothingness of human existence. Malivert had soon reached the chapel and not far from there, within a frame of Irish ivy, he saw the white tomb that had been made even whiter by a thin layer of snow. He leant over the railings and read the inscription engraved at the centre of the wreath of roses: 'Lavinia d'Aufideni, known in her life as a nun as Sister Philomène, died aged eighteen.' He extended his arm underneath the top railing and let his spray of lilacs fall on top of the inscription. Though he was sure of forgiveness, he stayed next to the grave for a few minutes in dreamy contemplation, his heart full of remorse. Had he not been the murderer of this pure dove that had returned so soon to heaven?

While he had been leaning on the railings around the monument, letting his tears flow and fall warm on to the cold snow that was the second shroud of the virgin's tomb, a break had formed in the thick curtain of grey clouds. In the same way as a light seen through layers of gauze appears less indistinct when the number of layers is reduced, so the disc of the sun changed from a pale white that looked more like the moon than the star of daylight to a true sun made for the dead! Little by little a gap appeared and through the opening there emerged a long ray of light visible against the dark misty background. It illuminated the spray of white lilacs and the wreath of marble roses and made them sparkle beneath the snowy mica as though it were a winter dew.

In the flickering ray of light, where a few frozen particles bobbed around, Malivert thought he could make out a slim white form rising from the grave, like a puff of smoke from a silver incense burner. It was wrapped in the floating folds of a gauze shroud like the robes in which painters clothe angels. And it waved a friendly hand towards him.

A cloud passed over the sun and the vision faded. Guy de Malivert walked away murmuring the name of Lavinia d'Aufideni. He got back into his carriage and returned to Paris, a city populated by living people who do not even suspect that, because they have no inner life, they are dead.

CHAPTER 13

From that day forth, Malivert's existence was split into two distinct parts, the one real, the other fantastical. To all appearances, he had not changed at all. He went to the club, he mixed in society; he was seen at the Bois de Boulogne and on the boulevard. If there was an interesting performance showing, he would be there and to see him well presented, wearing nice shoes and new gloves as he made his way through human life, no one would have suspected that this young man was in communication with the spirits or that when he came out of the Opéra, he glimpsed the mysterious depths of the invisible universe. If anyone had examined him closely, however, they would have found him more serious, paler, thinner and spiritualised, so to speak. The look in his eyes was no longer the same. When he was not distracted by conversation, they betrayed a kind of scornful bliss. Fortunately society only notices things in which it has an interest, and Malivert's secret was not suspected.

On the evening of his visit to the cemetery, when he had learnt Spirite's name on earth, he was waiting for a manifestation and was calling on all the strength of his willpower when, like drops of rain falling into a silver bowl, he heard a scale ring out on the piano. There was no one there, but these marvellous occurrences no longer shocked Malivert. A few chords were struck in order to attract attention and awaken the curiosity of his soul. Guy looked towards the piano, and gradually the charming shadow of a young girl took shape in a haze of light. The image was initially so transparent that the objects positioned behind her were visible through the outlines, as one sees the bottom of a lake through limpid water. Without taking on any material form, she then became sufficiently condensed to have the appearance of a living figure; but it was such a light, impalpable, ethereal life that she resembled the reflection of a body in a mirror more than the body itself. Some of Prud'hon's sketches give a vague idea of the graceful apparition sitting at Malivert's piano: they are lightly shaded with outlines that have been blurred and erased; they are bathed in a half-light and seem to be surrounded by a kind of twilight mist with white drapery that looks as though it were made of moonbeams. Her fingers were a very pale pink and they flitted over the ivory keyboard like white butterflies, just brushing the keys but evoking sound with a delicate touch that would not have disturbed the hairs of a feather. The notes did not need to be struck. Instead their sound rang out whenever her radiant hands fluttered over them. A long white dress, made of perfect muslin a thousand times finer than those pieces of Indian fabric that can pass through a wedding ring, fell in lavish folds around her and frothed at her toes in a frill of snowy lather. Her head was bent forward a little as though a score was open on the music stand and this meant the nape of her neck was visible covered with twisting golden waves and loose curls of stray hair; also revealed were the tips of pearly opaline shoulders, whose whiteness melted into that of the dress. Amongst the bands of cloth, quivering and puffed out as though by a breeze, there sparkled one studded strip whose ends were fastened behind her neck. From where Malivert was sitting, her ear and one corner of her cheek looked so pure and pink and velvety that they made the colours of a peach seem earthy. It was Lavinia, or Spirite to retain the name she has borne until now in this story. She turned her head around quickly to make sure Guy was paying attention and that she could begin. Her blue eyes shone with a tender light and had a celestial softness about them that pierced Guy's heart. There was still something of the girl in this angel's gaze.

The piece she played was the work of a great master, one of those inspired pieces in which human genius seems to have a foreboding of the infinite. At times they express the secret supplications of the soul; at others they remind it of heaven and paradise whence it was driven away. They breathe indescribable melancholy, gush fervent prayer and

145

make mute whispers audible. They are the last revolt of pride as it is plunged from light into darkness. Spirite conveyed all these sentiments with a mastery that made one forget keyboard magicians like Chopin, Listz and Thalberg. To Guy it seemed he was listening to music for the first time. A new art was being revealed to him and a thousand unknown notions moved about his soul. The notes awakened in him profound vibrations, so distant and ancient that he believed he had heard them in a previous life he had since forgotten. Not only did Spirite convey all that the composer intended but she expressed the ideal he dreamt of, which human infirmity had not always allowed him to attain. She supplemented genius, perfected perfection and added to the absolute.

Guy had stood up and walked over towards the piano like a sleepwalker who is unaware of the steps he is taking. He stood with his elbow on the corner of the piano case, his eyes plunged deep and passionately into Spirite's.

Spirite's face was truly sublime. Her head, which she had raised and thrown back a little, showed her face illuminated by the wonders of ecstasy. Inspiration and love shone with a supernatural sparkle in her eyes and her azure irises were almost disappearing from sight beneath her eyelids. Her half-open mouth let out a flash of gleaming pearl and her neck, bathed in blueish transparency like that of Guido's giant heads, was puffed out with pride like a mystical dove. The woman in her was diminishing and the angel increasing. And the intensity of light she was giving out was so strong that Malivert was forced to look away.

Spirite noticed this movement and, in a voice that was sweeter and more harmonious than the music she was playing, she whispered: 'My poor friend, I forgot that you are still held in your terrestrial prison and that your eyes cannot bear even the weakest ray of genuine light. In time I will appear to you as I am, in the sphere into which you will follow me. For now the shadow of my mortal form is enough to manifest my presence to you and that way you can gaze upon me without peril.'

By imperceptible transitions, she passed from supernatural

beauty back to natural beauty. The wings of Psyche, which for a moment had fluttered at her back, retreated into her white shoulders. Her immaterial appearance condensed a little and a milky cloud spread through the smooth outline of her body and reinforced it, as when one pours a drop of oil into water it makes the lines of the crystal that contain it easier to see. Lavinia was appearing again through Spirite; she was a little hazier certainly but sufficiently real to create the illusion.

She had stopped playing the piano and was looking at Malivert standing in front of her. A soft smile was hovering on her lips, a smile of celestial irony and divine malice, as she simultaneously mocked and soothed human weakness. Her eyes, which she had intentionally dulled, still expressed the tenderest love but in such a way that a chaste girl might have let it be seen on earth within an approved relationship. And for a few minutes Malivert was able to believe himself in the company of Lavinia, that girl who had sought him out so earnestly during her lifetime and from whom he had always been distanced by the quirks of fate. Frantic, bewitched and throbbing with love, forgetting that he only had a ghost before him, he moved forward and instinctively tried to take hold of one of Spirite's hands that still rested on the keyboard, and bring it to his lips. But his fingers closed around themselves, grasping nothing as if they had passed through fog.

Though she had nothing to fear, Spirite pulled away with a gesture that conveyed her insulted sense of propriety. Soon, however, her angelic smile returned and she raised her transparent hand of pink light up to the level of Guy's lips. And he sensed a kind of vague sweetness and smelt a delicate, delightful perfume.

'I wasn't thinking,' she said in a voice which did not express itself through words, but which Guy could hear in the depths of his heart. 'I wasn't thinking. I'm not a girl any more. I'm a soul now, a ghost, an impalpable vapour. I no longer have human senses and what Lavinia might perhaps have refused you Spirite grants you, not as a sensual pleasure but as a sign of pure love and eternal union' – and she allowed her fantastical hand to rest beneath Guy's imaginary kiss for several seconds.

She was soon at the piano again, making a melody of incomparable force and sweetness gush forth from the keyboard. In it Guy recognised one of his poems – his favourite – transposed from the language of verse into the language of music. It was an inspired poem in which, scornful of vulgar pleasures, he launched himself into a desperate flight towards the higher spheres where a poet's desire must ultimately be satisfied. With marvellous intuition, Spirite conveyed things that went beyond words, things that human language cannot express and so remain unsaid even in the best crafted phrase; she conveyed the mysteriousness, the intimacy and the profundity of things, the secret aspiration which one hardly admits to oneself, the unspeakable, the inexpressible, the *desideratum* of thoughts stretched to their limit, and the whole floating fuzzy mellow mass that spills out over the all too neat outline of the word. But with this flapping of wings which took her up into the azure blue with such unbridled momentum, she opened the paradise of dreams come true and hopes fulfilled. She stood on the threshold of illumination in a glittering atmosphere that would make suns look pale. She was divinely beautiful and yet humanly tender, opening her arms to the soul that had altered its ideal. She was both the goal and the reward, the crown of stars and the cup of love, a Beatrix that is only revealed beyond the grave. In a phrase drunk with the purest passion, she said with divine reticence and celestial modesty that in the freedom of eternity and the splendour of infinity she herself would quench all those unfulfilled desires. She promised his soul joy and love, but in such a way that human imagination, even when it is in touch with a spirit, could not conceive of them.

During this finale she had stood up. Her hands no longer gave the impression of brushing the keyboard and the tunes escaped from the piano in visible vibrations of colour that spread through the room's atmosphere in waves of light like the shades that tint the radiant explosions of the northern lights. Lavinia had disappeared and Spirite was reappearing but she was taller, more majestic and surrounded by a bright light. Long wings flapped at her shoulders and although she evidently wanted to stay she had already left the floor of the room. The folds of her dress floated in thin air. A greater inspiration was carrying her away and Malivert found himself alone again in a state of exaltation that is easy to understand. Gradually, however, he became calm once more and a delightful languor replaced that fevered excitement. He felt the kind of satisfaction that poets and philosophers, so they say, rarely experience. He felt that all the subtleties and profundities of his soul had been understood. What a glowing and dazzling commentary Spirite had made on that piece of poetry. Even he, as the author, had never understood its meaning and scope so clearly. How well that soul identified with his own! How well that mind penetrated his mind!

The next day he wanted to work. His creative zest, which had been inactive for a long time, now came to life again, and there was a tumultuous crush of ideas squeezed inside his brain. Limitless horizons and endless prospects opened up before his eyes. A world of new feelings was in a ferment in his breast and to express them he asked more of language than it can give. Old shapes and moulds were shattered and sometimes as the fluid phrase was being fused together it spurted out and overflowed but in wonderful splashes like rays of light from a shooting star. He had never risen to such heights and the greatest poets would have signed what he wrote that day.

With one verse finished, he mused on the next one. And as he did so, he let his eyes wander casually around the studio, and there half-lying on the divan he saw Spirite. She had her chin in her hand, her elbow buried in a cushion. The tips of her slender fingers were playing with her clouds of fair hair, and she was watching him with an air of loving contemplation. She seemed to have been there for a long time, but had not wanted to reveal her presence for fear of interrupting Guy's work. As Malivert was getting up out of his armchair to approach her, Spirite made a sign to him not to trouble himself. And in a voice that was sweeter than any music, she repeated verse for verse and line for line the piece Guy was working on. By some mysterious empathy, she sensed her lover's thoughts, followed them as they blossomed and even overtook them; for not only could she see but she could foresee; and she recited the whole of the unfinished stanza, an ending for which he was still seeking.

The work, as one might well imagine, was addressed to her. What other subject could Malivert have worked on? Carried along by his love for Spirite, he hardly had any recollection of earth and he plunged into the clear skies and went as high and as far as wings attached to human shoulders could take him.

'That is beautiful,' said Spirite and Malivert heard her voice resonate in his breast, for it did not reach his ears like ordinary sounds; 'even for a spirit that is beautiful; your genius is truly divine; it composes perfection and glimpses an eternal light and a higher beauty. To what heights will it not rise when it has faith and love for wings? Come back down, though. Come back to the place where the air can be breathed by mortal lungs. All your nerves are twitching like the strings of a lyre, your forehead is giving off steam like an incense burner and there is a strange excited gleam in your eyes. Ecstasy verges on madness, so be wary. Calm yourself and if you love me, go on living a human life.'

Obeying her, Malivert left his apartment and though men only seemed like distant shadows or ghosts with whom he no longer had any connection he tried to mix with them. He feigned interest in the day's news and gossip and smiled at the description of the phenomenal outfit Mademoiselle *** was wearing at the last Commoners' Ball. He even agreed to play a game of whist at the old duchess de C...'s. But he was indifferent to everything he did.

Yet despite his efforts to cling on to life, a pressing attraction was enticing him out of the earth's sphere. Whenever he tried to walk, he could feel himself rising up. An irresistible desire was eating away at him. Visions of Spirite were no longer enough for him and his soul would lunge after her whenever she disappeared, as though she had tried to detach herself from his body.

A love that was excited by its impossibility and that still burned with something of the terrestrial flame of desire devoured him and fastened on to his flesh as Nessus' poisoned tunic clung to the skin of Hercules. During that brief encounter with the Spirit, he had not been able to cast off completely his old human self.

He could not seize Spirite's ethereal phantom in his arms, but that phantom represented the image of Lavinia with an illusion of beauty sufficient to mislead his love and make him forget that this adorable form, with eyes full of tenderness and a voluptuous smiling mouth, was after all a mere ghost and a reflection.

At any time of the day or night, Guy could see before him the *alma adorata*, sometimes as a pure ideal through the splendour of Spirite, sometimes in the more humanly feminine guise of Lavinia. On some occasions, she would glide overhead in dazzling angelic flight; on others, like a visiting mistress, she would seem to be sitting in the great armchair or else stretched out on the divan or leaning on the table. She would appear to be looking at the papers spread out on the desk, or smelling the flowers in the window-boxes, opening the books or fiddling with the rings in the onyx cup on the mantelpiece. She looked as though she was absorbed in the kind of passionate childlike activities in which a girl indulges when she has wandered into her fiancé's room.

Spirite enjoyed manifesting herself before Guy's eyes, looking like Lavinia would have done, had fate looked favourably on her love. Posthumously and chapter by chapter, she reenacted her chaste boarding-school romance. With a puff of coloured smoke, she would reproduce her old costumes and put the same flower or ribbon in her hair. Her ghost would take on the grace, postures and poses of her virginal body. She showed an interest in her appearance that proved the woman had not totally disappeared in the angel. She wanted Malivert's love for her to be not just posthumous and directed at her spirit; she wanted him to love her as she was

151

during her life on earth, when she used to be at the Italiens, at a ball, or in society, seeking – but always missing – the chance to see him.

In a transport of desire, madly in love and drunk with passion, Guy would occasionally forget himself and indulge in some pointless caress, but the vision was something so clear, colourful and alive that if his lips had not touched thin air, he could well have believed that he, Guy de Malivert, had really married Lavinia d'Aufideni. In a perfect blend of mutual empathy, he would hear Lavinia's voice with its young fresh silvery tone inside himself, but as though he were listening to a real conversation. She would reply to his passionate outbursts with chaste and modest tenderness.

It really was the torture of Tantalus. The cup full of frozen water would approach his burning lips held by a loving hand, but he could not even touch the rim. The sweet-smelling, amber-coloured grapes hung down over his head and then rose out of reach, fleeing an impossible embrace.

The short intervals during which Spirite left him, having been recalled no doubt by some ineluctable order to 'that place where you can do what you want to do' had become unbearable for him. Whenever she disappeared, he would happily have smashed his skull against the wall that closed around her.

One evening, he said to himself: 'Spirite cannot don a body or involve herself in my life other than through visions, so what if I were to cast off this troublesome mortal shell, this thick, heavy shape that is preventing me from rising up with the soul I adore to the realms where souls soar?'

It seemed to him that this was a wise resolution. He stood up and went over to a display of primitive weapons that hung on the wall. There were clubs, tomahawks, assegais and cutlasses. He picked out an arrow feathered with parrot feathers and fitted with a fishbone tip. The arrow had been dipped in *curare*, that awful poison whose secret is known only to the American Indians: it strikes its victims and no antidote can save them.

He held the arrow close to his hand, about to prick it

when Spirite suddenly appeared before him. She was frantic, alarmed, pleading; and she threw her ghostly arms around his neck with a lunge of mad passion, clutching him to her phantom's heart and covering him with impalpable kisses. The woman had forgotten she was now only a spirit.

'You poor man,' she cried out. 'Don't do that. Don't kill yourself to be reunited with me. If your death were brought on in this way, it would separate us hopelessly. It would dig an abyss between us that millions of years would not be long enough to cross. Take hold of yourself. Put up with life. Even the longest life lasts no longer than the time it takes for a grain of sand to fall. To cope with time, dream of eternity, when we will always be able to love each other. And forgive me for having been flirtatious. The woman in me wanted to be loved like the spirit. Lavinia was jealous of Spirite and I almost lost you for ever.'

Reassuming her angelic form, she stretched her hands out over Malivert's head and he felt a celestial coolness descend upon him.

CHAPTER 14

Madame d'Ymbercourt was shocked at how little effect her coquettishness towards Monsieur d'Aversac had had on Guy de Malivert. Her lack of success shattered all her ideas on feminine wiles. She thought that nothing revived love better than jealousy, but she was forgetting that for the adage to be true, love had to exist. Given that this young man had come quite regularly to her Wednesday soirées for three years, had sometimes brought her a bouquet on days when there was a performance at the Italiens, and had stayed at the back of her box without falling asleep, she was unlikely to think he was not a little taken with her charms. Was she not young and beautiful, and elegant and rich? Did she not play the piano like the winner of a first prize from the Conservatoire? Did she not pour tea with the correctness of Lady Penelope herself? Did she not write her morning notelets in an English hand that was tall, slanting, angular and thoroughly aristocratic? How could one criticise her carriages? They came from Binder's. And her horses were sold to her and guaranteed by Crémieux. Were her servants not well-built? Were they not like those servants at the big houses? And did her dinners not deserve a gourmet's approval? All of this seemed to her to make for quite a reasonable ideal.

However, her memory of the lady she had glimpsed in the sleigh at the Bois de Boulogne kept running through her mind and on several occasions she had gone for a walk around the lake with the idea she might come across her and see if Malivert was following her. But the lady never appeared again and Madame d'Ymbercourt's jealousy was left to play itself out in a void. What was worse, no one knew her or had noticed her. Was Guy in love with her? Or had he merely yielded to an impulse of curiosity when he had launched Grymalkin in pursuit of the trotter? That is what Madame d'Ymbercourt could not work out. So she came back to the idea that she had angered Guy by making him think he had compromised her reputation. She had said what she had said to force him to make a formal declaration, but now she regretted it. For Guy, who had obeyed her orders too closely, and moreover was busy with Spirite, had refrained from visiting her altogether. This perfect obedience annoyed the countess; she would have preferred him to be less submissive. Although her suspicions were only founded on the brief sighting in the Bois de Boulogne, she sensed there was a love affair hiding behind this excessive concern for her reputation. Yet to all appearances, nothing had changed in Guy's life. And when Jack was secretly interrogated by Madame d'Ymbercourt's maid, he assured her it had been a good while since he had heard the slightest rustle of silk on his master's staircase. He went out rarely and hardly saw anyone except the baron de Féroë. He lived the life of a monk and spent a large portion of his nights writing.

D'Aversac became even more attentive and Madame d'Ymbercourt accepted this with the kind of tacit gratitude of a woman who is a little neglected and needs to be reassured of her charms by new admirers. She did not love Monsieur d'Aversac but she was grateful to him for prizing so highly what Guy seemed to be spurning. And so, on the Tuesday at a performance of *La Traviata*, people remarked that Malivert's seat was occupied by d'Aversac, in white tie and gloves, with a camellia in his button-hole, his hair curled and pomaded like a wealthy man and sparkling, like everything about him, with a happy self-conceit. He had nurtured the ambition to be liked by Madame d'Ymbercourt for a long time. But the marked preference she had shown for Guy de Malivert had pushed him back to the third or fourth rank of distant admirers who revolve at various points around a pretty woman, waiting for an opportunity or a break-up or a fit of pique that never comes.

He was full of little shows of thoughtfulness. He passed the opera-glasses or the programme, smiled at the least remark, leant towards her secretively to answer questions and when Madame d'Ymbercourt brought the tips of her white gloves

155

together to sound her approval at some extended note in the diva's performance, he applauded enough to bring the house down, lifting up his hands level with his head. In short, he was publicly taking up his role as escort.

People in some boxes were already saying: 'Is the marriage between Malivert and Madame d'Ymbercourt not going ahead?' There was a burst of curiosity when, after the first act, Guy appeared at the entrance to the stalls and could be seen examining the auditorium and looking casually at the countess's box. D'Aversac, who had spotted Guy, experienced a slight feeling of unease, but the most perceptive opera-glasses could not have made out the slightest sign of annoyance on Malivert's face. He did not blush or grow pale. He did not screw up his eyebrows. Not one facial muscle moved. He was not seen with that awful expression that jealous lovers assume when confronted with the sight of their beautiful mistress with another man. He looked calm and perfectly serene. His facial expression was the kind brought about by the radiance of a secret feeling of joy and, as the poet says, there hovered on his lips:

> The mysterious smile
> Of an inner pleasure.

'Guy couldn't look more elated, even if he were loved by a fairy or a princess,' said an old and practised Don Juan who was a regular visitor to the dress circle. 'If Madame d'Ymbercourt has her heart set on this marriage she's hoping for, then it's time for her to go into mourning because she will never be called Madame de Malivert.'

During the interval, Guy made a brief visit to the countess's box to bid her farewell. He was going to travel for a few months in Greece. His politeness with d'Aversac was natural, with no sign of annoyance or exaggeration. He did not appear cold and ceremonious as a vexed person might and he shook Madame d'Ymbercourt's hand perfectly gently. Her distress was given away by her bearing, despite her efforts to appear indifferent. The blush that had coloured her cheeks when Guy had left his seat in the stalls to come to the box, had been replaced by a paleness in which her powder puff had played no part. She was hoping for a fit of pique, an outburst of passion, a sign of jealousy or perhaps even a quarrel. This coolness was no act and it disconcerted and surprised her. She had thought that Malivert loved her and now she saw that she had been wrong. This discovery wounded both her pride and her heart. She was more acutely fond of Guy than she had thought and she felt unhappy. The act she was putting on, now that it no longer served any purpose, made her feel irritated and weary. When Malivert had left, she leant her elbows on the edge of the box and only responded in monosyllables to the gallant remarks d'Aversac addressed to her. This silence and coldness troubled him. Though he could not explain it, spring had turned to winter. A sudden frost covered the roses: 'Have I done or said something stupid?' wondered the poor young man, who not long ago had been so welcome. 'Or is everyone, by any chance, making fun of me? Guy's relaxed manner just now seemed affected and the countess seemed extremely moved. Could it be that she still loves Malivert?' However, as d'Aversac knew he was the focus of a number of pairs of opera-glasses, he continued playing his role, leaning towards the countess and whispering banal remarks in her ear. Anyone might have listened to them but he whispered them in an intimate and mysterious way.

The old regular was amused by this little drama and he followed its plot out of the corner of his eye. 'D'Aversac's making a hash of looking cheerful. He's not good enough to play this part. He's a fool, though. And fools are sometimes lucky with women. Foolishness and madness understand each other well and Laridon takes over from Caesar mainly because Caesar wants nothing more to do with his empire. But who can Guy's new mistress be?' These were the musings of this veteran Cytherean, who was as strong on theory as he had been in practice. He followed Malivert's gaze to see if he was not staring at one of the beautiful creatures who were glittering in the boxes like jewels in their case. 'Might it be that misty blonde wearing the garland of silver flowers, the aquamarine dress and the set of pearls? She looks as though her make-up were done with moonbeams, like an elf or a water-nymph. She's gazing sentimentally at the chandelier as though it were the evening star. Or perhaps it's that brunette with hair darker than the night, a profile cut in marble, eyes made of black diamonds and a crimson mouth. She is so vivacious beneath her warm paleness, so passionate beneath her statuesque calm. You'd think she was the daughter of the Venus de Milo, if that divine masterpiece had deigned to have children. No, it's not either of them – neither the moon nor the sun. That Russian princess over there in the stage box, with her mad luxury, her exotic beauty and her excessive grace, she might be in with a chance. Guy quite likes strange things and because of his travels he has somewhat barbaric tastes. No, it's not her. He just looked at her with eyes as cold as if he were examining a trunk of malachite. Why not that Parisian woman in the open box; she's dressed perfectly tastefully. She's so fine, so cheerful, so pretty; her every movement looks as though it is following the sound of a flute, and it lifts up a froth of lace as though she were dancing on a panel in Herculaneum. Balzac would have devoted thirty pages to describing such a woman. And that would have been no misuse of style: she's worth it. But Guy isn't civilised enough to taste the kind of charm that seduced, more than beauty itself, the author of the *Comédie Humaine*. Ah well, I'll have to give up trying to solve this mystery today,' said the handsome old man, as he put back into their case a pair of opera-glasses that looked more like a gun. 'The lady in Malivert's thoughts is clearly not here.'

At the exit, d'Aversac was standing below the columns with all the elegance a gentleman can assume when he is wrapped up in his overcoat. Next to him was Madame d'Ymbercourt who had thrown over her outfit a satin pelisse trimmed with swan's down; her hood was draped over her shoulders leaving her head bare. The countess was pale and that evening she was truly beautiful. The pain she was feeling gave her face, normally so cold and straight, a certain expression and life that had been lacking until now. Moreover, she seemed to have completely forgotten about her suitor, who stayed two steps behind her. He retained a composed gravity and strove both to hide and to say a great deal.

'What has happened to Madame d'Ymbercourt this evening?' said the young people who had positioned themselves in the foyer in order to put together a critique of the women. 'It's as though a new kind of beauty has come over her. D'Aversac is a lucky rascal.'

'Not as lucky as all that,' said a young man with a fine cheerful face, who looked like a Van Dyck portrait removed from its frame. 'The countess's face is usually as inexpressive as a wax mask moulded on a Venus by Canova. It isn't he who has given it such animation and character. Her sparkle comes from elsewhere. D'Aversac isn't this Pandora's Prometheus. Wood couldn't bring marble to life.'

'That's right,' another man went on. 'It's quite sickening that Malivert should leave the countess now. She deserves better than d'Aversac as her avenger. I don't know whether Guy will find a better woman but he might well regret his disdainful attitude.'

'He'd be wrong to regret it,' replied the Van Dyck portrait. 'Follow my reasoning carefully. Madame d'Ymbercourt is more beautiful than normal today because she's emotional. Now, if Malivert weren't to leave her, she would feel no emotion, her classically regular features would retain their insignificance and the phenomenon you now remark would not be taking place. So Malivert would be wise to go off to Greece, just like he announced yesterday at the club. And that's the end of the matter.'

The footman calling for the countess's carriage put an end to this conversation and more than one young man experienced a sinful feeling of envy seeing d'Aversac climb into the grand coupé after Madame d'Ymbercourt. The carriage door was closed behind him by the servant who, in the twinkle of an eye, had climbed up on to the driver's seat. The carriage set off at a rapid pace. D'Aversac was so close to this woman that he was half-covered with a cascade of satin. He breathed in the vague perfume that emanated from her, and tried to make the most of this brief tête-à-tête to say a few words to the countess that were a little more tender and loving. He had to find something authoritative and passionate to say straight away: it is not far from Place Ventadour to Rue de la Chaussée d'Antin. But improvisation was not the forte of Guy's rival. Madame d'Ymbercourt, it must be said, scarcely encouraged him. She was silent and curled up in the corner of the coupé, nibbling at the corner of her lace-trimmed handkerchief.

While d'Aversac was doing his best to complete a laboured loving phrase, Madame d'Ymbercourt was not listening to a word. She was entirely taken up with pursuing her own line of thought. Suddenly she took his arm and said to him curtly: 'Do you know Monsieur de Malivert's new mistress?'

This strange, unexpected question shocked d'Aversac considerably. It was in dubious taste and it proved to him that the countess had not been thinking about him for one moment. His hopes were a house of cards that collapsed in the face of this breath of passion.

'I do not know her,' stammered d'Aversac. 'And if I did, discretion and politeness ... would prevent me ... In such circumstances any decent man knows his duty...'

'Yes, of course,' the countess continued in a jerky tone. 'Men all stick together, even when they are rivals. I could not ...' Then, after a short silence, she took hold of herself a little, and said: 'I'm sorry, my dear Monsieur d'Aversac, my nerves are terribly on edge. I realise I'm saying ridiculous things. Don't hold it against me. Come and see me tomorrow. I'll be calmer then. Here we are, anyway,' she said holding out her hand to him. 'Where do you need to be taken?' And she scurried out of the coupé and climbed the steps to her house, keen that d'Aversac should not help her.

Clearly, it is not always as pleasant as naive young people imagine to accompany a beautiful young lady home in a carriage from the Italiens to Chaussée d'Antin. Feeling somewhat sheepish, d'Aversac had himself taken to the club in Rue de Choiseul, where his driver was waiting for him. He gambled and lost about a hundred louis, which did not help put him in a good mood. As he was going home, he said to himself: 'How does that devil Malivert manage to make women love him like that?'

Madame d'Ymbercourt gave herself over to the care and attentions of her maid, who undressed her and prepared her for bed. Then she wrapped herself in a white cashmere dressing gown and leant her elbows on her desk with her hand buried in her hair. She stayed like this for some time, with her eyes staring at her sheet of paper, rolling her pen between her fingers. She wanted to write to Guy but this would be a difficult letter to produce. Thoughts that came to her in a tumult vanished when she tried to enclose them in a sentence. She scribbled five or six drafts that were covered with crossings out and were illegible despite her beautiful English handwriting; and still she was not satisfied. Some of them said too much; the others said too little. None of them conveyed the sentiments of her heart. All of them were ripped up and thrown on to the fire. She finally settled on this version:

'Do not be angry, my dear Guy, at my flirtatious behaviour. It was quite innocent, I swear to you, for its only aim was to make you a little jealous and bring you back to me. You know quite well that I love you, though you don't exactly love me. Your attitude is so cold and calm and it has turned my heart to ice. Forget what I told you. A spiteful friend of mine made me say it. About this trip to Greece... is it true? Do you need so much to flee from me? All I want to do is please you. Don't go away. Your absence would make me too unhappy.'

The countess signed this note 'Cécile d'Ymbercourt' sealed it with her coat of arms and wanted to send it off on the spot. But as she was getting up to call for someone, the clock struck two: it was too late to send a man to the far side of the district of Saint-Germain where Guy lived. 'It's alright,' she said, 'I'll send my letter early in the morning and

Guy will have it when he wakes, provided he hasn't already left.'

She went to bed, tired and brokenhearted, and it was in vain that she shut her eyes. She thought of the woman in the sleigh and told herself that Malivert loved *her* and jealousy drove its fine needles into her heart. Finally she fell asleep but it was a restless sleep filled with convulsions that were more painful than they had been during the day. A little lamp, which served as a night light and hung from the ceiling enclosed in a globe of blue frosted glass, diffused an azure glow through the room quite similar to the glow of moonlight. It shone a sweet mysterious light on to the countess's head. Her hair was loose and it had fallen in big black curls on to the white pillow. And she had let one of her arms hang out of the bed.

At the head of the bed, a light vapour, transparent and blue like the smoke that comes from a perfume burner, gradually condensed. The vapour took on a clearer shape and soon it became a young girl of celestial beauty with golden hair that made a brilliant halo. Spirite, for it was she, watched the young woman sleep with that air of melancholic piety that angels must have in the face of human suffering. Leaning towards her like the shadow of a dream, she poured on to her forehead two or three drops of a dark liquid that was held inside a little ewer similar to those tear-bottles found in ancient tombs. As she did this, she whispered: 'You no longer pose a threat to the man I love and you can no longer separate his soul from mine. I feel sorry for you now. You are suffering because of him. I've brought you a draught of divine nepenthes. Forget him and be happy, you who caused my death.'

The vision disappeared. The features of the sleeping beauty relaxed as if an unpleasant nightmare had given way to a sweet dream. A slight smile hovered on her lips. In an unconscious movement, she brought back into the bed her beautiful bare arm that had taken on the coldness of marble to match the whiteness it already had; and she snuggled up under the light eiderdown. Her calm, refreshing sleep lasted

162

until morning and when she woke, the first thing she noticed was her letter placed on the bedside table.

'Should I have this sent?' said Aglaé, who had just come into the room to open the curtains and could see her mistress's eyes focussing on the missive. 'Oh no!' exclaimed Madame d'Ymbercourt sharply. 'Throw it on the fire.' Then she added to herself: 'What was I thinking of to write such a letter? I must have been mad.'

CHAPTER 15

The steamer making the trip between Marseilles and Athens had drawn level with Cape Malea, the last indentation in that mulberry leaf which forms the tip of Greece and has given it its modern name. They had left behind the clouds, the fog and the wintry weather. They were passing from darkness into light, from cold into warmth. The grey tones of the Western sky had given way to the azure of the Eastern sky and the deep blue sea undulated gently in a favourable breeze. The steamer had made the most of this by unfurling its smoke-blackened jibs; they were like the dark-coloured sails that Theseus hoisted by mistake on his return from vanquishing the minotaur on the island of Crete. February was nearing its close and the approach of spring, which comes so late at home, could already be felt in this lucky sun-loved climate. The air was so warm that most of the passengers, being already hardened against seasickness, stayed up on the bridge and were busy looking at the coast that could be glimpsed through the blue haze of the evening. Above this gloomy area, a mountain rose up, still visible. There was still a ray of sunlight on its glistening snow-capped peak. It was Mount Taygetus. It gave those passengers who were Bachelors of Arts and knew a few snatches of Latin, the opportunity to cite with smug pedantry Virgil's well-known line of poetry. A Frenchman who can aptly quote a line of Latin poetry is a rare thing and it comes very close to making him blissfully happy. As for quoting a line of Greek, that is a joy reserved for Germans or Englishmen who have been to Jena or Oxford.

On the slatted benches and folding stools that cluttered the rear of the ship sat young English governesses wearing little hats with blue veils, over thick red hair enclosed in nets. Travelling bags hung from straps around their necks and they were dressed in big-buttoned overcoats. They gazed at the coast, hazy in the evening darkness, through binoculars that were strong enough to make out the satellites around Jupiter. The more daring amongst them, having seafaring legs, walked back and forth along the bridge with the gymnastic step that drill sergeants and walking instructors teach young ladies from across the Channel. Some of them chatted to perfectly decent gentlemen of impeccable appearance. There were French people too, pupils from the college in Athens, painters, architects who had won the Prix de Rome and were going to soak up the source of true beauty. These people had all the drive of youth that comes from having hope ahead of one and a few savings in one's pocket. They joked and laughed loudly, they smoked cigars and indulged in heated discussions about aesthetics. The reputations of the great masters, ancient and modern, were discussed and either repudiated or praised to the skies. Everything was either admirable or ridiculous, sublime or stupid, for young people are excessive and know no middle ground. *They* would not marry King Modus and Queen Ratio. That marriage of convenience only happens later in life.

Amid this lively group, with his coat draped about him like a Stoic, was a young man, who was neither painter nor sculptor nor architect and whom the travelling artists used as an arbiter when a discussion ended up in some stubborn negation from both sides. It was Guy de Malivert. His fine, judicious remarks showed him to be a true connoisseur, an art critic worthy of the title, and these young people who were so contemptuous and branded everyone who has not worked with a brush, a chisel or a drawing pen, with the epithet bourgeois, listened to those remarks with a certain deference and sometimes even heeded them. But the conversation dried up, as everything dries up – even a conversation on idealism and reality – and the people who had been talking found their throats a little dry. They went down into the saloon to refresh their hoarse voices with some hot toddy or some other warm and hearty beverage. Malivert stayed alone on the bridge. Night had completely fallen. In the dark azure sky, the stars shone with a sparkle so bright and brilliant that it could only be imagined if one has not seen the sky in Greece. Their reflections stretched out in the water, forming a trail, as lights on the shore would have done. The froth thrown up by the paddle-wheels splashed up in millions of diamonds that shone for a moment and then melted into a blueish phosphorescence. The dark steamer seemed to be swimming in a pool of light. It was the kind of spectacle that would inspire the admiration of the most obtuse Philistine and Malivert, who was no Philistine, found it delightfully exquisite. It did not even occur to him to go down to the steerage where there always prevails a nauseating warmth that is particularly noticeable when one comes in from the fresh air. He continued to stroll from the rear of the ship to the front, dodging the Levantines who had settled along the boards at the bow, on their rugs or their thin mattresses, amid piles of chains and rolls of rope. Occasionally he caused a woman to lower her veil; having thought she was not being watched, she had lifted it up to inhale the fresh night air. Guy, as one can see, was keeping the promise he had made not to sully Madame d'Ymbercourt's reputation. He leant on the ship's rail and gave himself over to a dream full of sweetness. Certainly, since Spirite's love had freed him from the earth's curiosities, the trip to Greece no longer inspired in him the same enthusiasm it once had. He would have liked to have taken a different kind of trip but he no longer considered speeding up his departure for that world in which his thoughts were already immersed. He knew now the consequences of suicide and without too much impatience he awaited the day when he would fly off with the angel that was visiting him. Assured of his future happiness, he indulged in immediate sensation and as a poet he relished the magnificent spectacle of the night. Like Lord Byron, he loved the sea. Its perpetual restlessness and its moaning – even at the calmest times it was never silent, its sudden uprisings and its insane fits of anger against immovable obstacles, had always appealed to his imagination, which saw in this vain turbulence a secret analogy with the pointlessness of human effort. What appealed to him above all about the sea was the vast isolation; the way the circle of the horizon always looked the same, always out of place; the solemn monotony; and the absence of any sign of civilisation. The same swell that lifted up the steamer on a great wave had washed up against the 'low-sided' vessels that Homer speaks of, and no trace of it remained. The water had precisely the same hue as when the Greek fleet cut a wake through it. The sea is proud and does not bear the scars of man's passage as the earth does. It is as hazy and huge and deep as infinity. So Malivert never felt more cheerful, free or in control of himself than when he stood at the prow of a ship rising and falling and advancing into the unknown. Soaked by the lashing froth that splashed up on to the bridge, his hair impregnated with the salty vapour, it seemed to him that he was walking on water. And as a horseman relates to the speed of his mount, so he took on the vessel's speed and his thoughts leapt ahead of the waves.

Near Malivert, Spirite had come down soundlessly like a feather or a snowflake, and her hand rested on the young man's shoulder. Although Spirite was invisible to everybody, one can well imagine the charming couple that Malivert and his ethereal friend made. The moon was up, big and bright, making the stars look pale, and the night had become a kind of blue day, a day that was an azure grotto with a truly magical hue. A beam of light picked out this Eros and this Psyche at the prow of the ship, shining in the diamond sparkle of the froth like young gods at the prow of an ancient bireme. A wide trail of silver specks stretched over the sea in a perpetual swarm of light. This was the reflection of the star that had risen up from the horizon and was slowly climbing up through the sky. Occasionally a black-backed dolphin, a descendant perhaps of the one that carried Arion, would swim across the sparkling wake, before returning swiftly to the shadows. Or in the distance, like a quivering red dot, the lantern on some small boat would be seen. From time to time, the coastline of an island would appear like a violet outline, soon to be left behind.

'That,' said Spirite, 'is unquestionably a marvellous sight

and one of the most beautiful, if not *the* most beautiful, that the human eye may gaze upon. But what is it alongside the fantastic sights of the world I have left to come down to you, and where we will soon fly next to one another 'like doves summoned by the same desire'? This sea, which seems to you so great, is only a drop in the cup of infinity and that pale star that illuminates it is an imperceptible silver globule, which would get lost in the frightening immensity of space like the last grain of astral dust. Oh, how I would have admired this spectacle if I had been next to you when I still lived on earth and was called Lavinia. But don't think that I'm insensitive to it; I can understand its beauty through your emotion.'

'How impatient you make me for the other life, Spirite,' Malivert replied. 'How keen I am to set off for those worlds of dazzling splendours greater than anything that could be imagined or put into words, worlds we will travel through together where nothing will ever separate us again.'

'Yes, you will see them. You will come to know their munificence and their delights, as long as you love me and are faithful to me and your thoughts don't get diverted to anything inferior; as long as you drop the vulgar, impure silt of humanity to the bottom of yourself as though to the bottom of a pool of still water. If you pay this price, we will be eternally united with one another and we will be allowed to savour the peaceful intoxication of divine love, the kind of love that never rests, never weakens and never tires; its ardour would melt suns like grains of myrrh in a fire. We shall be unity within duality, the me within the not-me, action within rest, desire within fulfilment, coolness within the flame. To deserve this supreme bliss, dream of Spirite in the sky, and don't dwell too much on memories of Lavinia. She sleeps beneath that wreath of sculpted white roses.'

'Do I not love you madly?' said Malivert 'and with all the purity and ardour of which a soul still captive on this earth can be capable?'

168

'My friend,' replied Spirite, 'stay that way. I am happy with you.'

And as she said these words, her sapphire eyes twinkled full of loving promises, and a voluptuously chaste smile half opened her adorable mouth.

The exchange between the living man and the ghost continued until the first glow of dawn had begun to merge its pink hue into the violet shades of the moon, whose disc was gradually disappearing. Soon a segment of the sun appeared above the dark blue bar that the sea formed on the horizon and the day overflowed in a sublime explosion. Spirite was an angel of light and had nothing to fear from the sun. And she stayed for a few minutes at the prow, sparkling with pink light while the fiery glow of morning played like golden butterflies in her hair as it was blown out by the Archipelago breeze. If she preferred to choose the night-time to make her apparitions, it was because that was when the mundane activity of human life was broken off. Guy was then at greater liberty and less under scrutiny; and he did not have to run risk of passing for a madman because of actions that were necessarily bizarre in appearance.

Seeing Malivert pale and frozen in the chill of dawn, she said to him in a scolding but gentle tone: 'Come on, you poor clay creature, don't fight nature. It's cold, the sea's dew is drenching the bridge and soaking the rigging. Go back into the cabin, go and sleep.' And then she added with a charm that was entirely feminine: 'Sleep doesn't separate us. I'll be in all your dreams, and I'll lead you to the places you can't yet get to when you're awake.'

And indeed Guy's sleep was filled with dreams that were azure blue and dazzling and supernatural, where he flew side by side with Spirite across Elysian fields and heavens. There was a perfect blend of light and vegetation and architecture. And no phrase in any of our wretched languages, so restricted and imperfect and opaque as they are, could evoke even the vaguest idea of it.

It is pointless to describe the impressions of Malivert's journey in detail. That would be to venture outside the frame of this story. And besides Guy was preoccupied with his love and distracted by an inexorable desire. He was paying far less attention than before to material things. He could only glimpse nature now as something vague, hazy and wondrous in the distance, which served as the backcloth for his obsession. For him, the world was only a landscape for Spirite and even then, he found the finest beauty spots scarcely worthy of this role.

However, the following day at sunrise he could not help crying out in admiration and surprise when the steamer entered the harbour at Piraeus and he caught sight of the marvellous tableau that lit up the morning. Parnassus and Hymettus, with their amethyst-coloured slopes, were like the wings of a wonderful stage set. Lycabetus, with its strangely jagged outline, and Pentelicus occupied the background. In the middle, like a golden tripod on a marble altar, the Parthenon, illuminated by the morning's vermilion glow, rose up on top of the Acropolis. The blueish tones of the distant landscape, that appeared through the spaces between the ruined columns, made the noble form of the temple even more ethereal and perfect. Malivert felt the thrill that beauty inspires and he understood things that until now had seemed obscure. In this brief vision, all of Greek art was revealed to him, the romantic: the perfect proportion of the whole, the absolute purity of the lines, the incomparable smoothness of the colour made up of whiteness, azure blue and light.

As soon as he had disembarked, and without worrying about his luggage which he left to Jack to take care of, he jumped into one of those fiacres which, in the absence of ancient chariots, put modern civilisation to shame as they carry passengers from Piraeus to Athens on a dusty white road lined here and there with a few dust-covered olive trees. Malivert's vehicle was falling apart and it made a worrying rattling noise. It was drawn along at a gallop by two thin little horses, dapple-grey in colour, with their manes sticking up and cut in a brush-like style. They were like the skeletons, or rather earthenware models, of the marble horses that rear up on the metopes of the Parthenon; their ancestors no doubt posed for Phidias. They were being flogged ferociously by a youth dressed in a Palikar outfit, who long ago might have won the prize for chariot racing at Olympia, had he been driving a finer team of horses.

Leaving the other travellers to invade the Hôtel d'Angleterre, Guy got himself taken to the foot of the sacred hill where the human race, in the flower of its youth, poetry and love, piled up its purest masterpieces as though to present them for the admiration of the gods. He went up the old Street of the Tripods, that lies buried beneath shapeless huts, treading respectfully underfoot that dust made of marvellous things. He finally came out on to the staircase to the Propylaea, whose steps have been taken up to make tombstones. He climbed through this strange cemetery, walking amid a mess of raised slabs and foundations, one of which supports the little temple of the Wingless Victory, the other acting both as a pedestal for the equestrian statue by Cimon and as a terrace in front of the Pinakotheke, which is where masterpieces by Zeuxis, Apelles, Timanthes and Protogenes were kept.

He passed with a sense of religious admiration through the Propylaea, designed by Mnesicles, itself a masterpiece worthy of its role as a gateway on to the masterpiece created by Ictinus and Phidias. As a barbaric Westerner, he was almost ashamed to be walking in boots over this sacred soil.

After a few steps, he found himself in front of the Parthenon – temple of the Virgin – sanctuary of Pallas-Athene, and the purest creation of polytheism.

The edifice spread out in the serene blue air, superbly placid and majestically calm. A divine harmony presided over those lines as they sang the hymn of beauty to a secret rhythm. They all veered smoothly towards an unknown ideal, converging towards a mysterious point but doing so without effort or strain, as though they were sure they would reach it. Above the temple, one felt this idea was hovering and it seemed that the corners of the pediments, the entablatures and the columns were aspiring towards it, that they wanted to rise up to it, projecting invisible curves beyond the horizontal and the perpendicular. The beautiful Doric columns, draped in the folds of their fluting and set back a little, inspired dreams of chaste virgins feeling languid with a vague notion of desire.

A light warm colour enveloped the facade in a golden atmosphere and the kiss of time had lent the marble a vermilion hue that was like a blush of modesty.

On the steps to the temple, between two columns – behind which the gate opens on to the pronaos – stood Spirite. In that pure Greek light, so unsuitable for apparitions, on the very threshold of the Parthenon, so bright and perfect and beautifully luminous, she wore a long white dress with little sculpted folds like the tunics of the canephorae, that stretched from her shoulders right to the tips of her little bare feet. A crown of violets – those same violets whose freshness Aristophenes celebrates in one of his dramatic choruses – encircled the wavy locks of her golden hair. In this outfit, Spirite looked like a virgin from the Panathenaeon, who had climbed down from her frieze. But in her periwinkle blue eyes shone a softened glow that cannot be seen in eyes of white marble. To that radiant plastic beauty, she added the beauty of the soul.

Malivert climbed the steps and approached Spirite, who held out her hand towards him. And in a brief flash of light, he saw the Parthenon as it was in its days of splendour. The fallen columns had taken up their positions again. The figures from the facade, stolen by Lord Elgin, or shattered by Venetian bombs, were grouped together on the facades. They were pure, intact and caught in poses that were humanly divine. Through the gateway to the cella, Malivert caught a glimpse of Phidias's statue of gold and ivory perched on its pedestal: the celestial woman, the virgin, the immaculate Pallas-Athene. But he only gave this wonderful sight a casual glance and his eyes immediately sought Spirite.

Spurned in this way, the vision of the past disappeared.

'Oh!' whispered Spirite. 'Even art is forgotten for love. His soul is gradually freeing itself from the earth. He's burning up. He's wasting away. Soon, dear soul, your wish will be granted!'

And with the girl's heart still beating inside the spirit's breast, a sigh lifted up her white peplum.

CHAPTER 16

A few days after his visit to the Parthenon, Guy de Malivert resolved to go on a tour of the area around Athens and visit those beautiful mountains he could see from his window. He took a guide and two horses and left Jack at the hotel. It would have been pointless, and awkward even, for him to have come. Jack was one of those servants that are more difficult to please than their masters and whose bothersome ways are only revealed when they are travelling. He had the habits of an old spinster and thought everything was dreadful – the rooms, the beds, the food and the wine. He was constantly outraged by the barbarism of the service and would exclaim: 'Oh! They're so uncivilised.' Furthermore, though he might have recognised in Malivert a certain talent for writing, deep down he judged him to be incapable of controlling himself and a little mad, especially recently. He had given himself the task of watching over him. A frown from Malivert, however, made him shrink back from his intentions and his marvellous talent for metamorphosis saw the mentor take up the role of valet once more.

Guy slipped a number of gold coins into a leather belt he was wearing under his clothes and put pistols into the holsters on his saddle. When he set off, he did not fix a precise date for his return, as he wanted to leave himself the freedom to roam aimlessly and encounter unforeseen adventures. He knew that Jack, who was used to his disappearing, would not get alarmed if he was a few days or even a few weeks late. He would be perfectly happy once he had taught the hotel chef to cook steak according to his ideas: quickly, so the outside was well done and the inside was pink, in the English style.

Guy's trip, provided he did not change his plans, was to be limited to Parnassus and was not supposed to be longer than five or six days. But after a month, neither Malivert nor his guide had reappeared. No letter had come to the hotel to announce a change or lengthening of the itinerary. The money Guy had taken with him would be running out and this silence was beginning to worry Jack. 'Monsieur hasn't asked me for money,' he said to himself one morning, as he ate a steak that was at last properly cooked, and washed it down with a Santorin white wine that was quite pleasant despite its slight taste of resin. 'Something's not right. Something must have happened to him. If he was continuing his trip, he would have given me the name of a town so I could send him some money, since it's me that's in charge of the finances ... That is, if he hasn't broken his neck or his back falling down a precipice! What kind of devilish notion is it, anyway, that makes him always go off on horseback around countries that are dirty, badly cobbled, absurd and miserable, when we could be in Paris, tucked up snugly in some comfortable place, protected from insects and mosquitoes and the other awful creatures that bring you out in blisters? I don't mean in the summer months. Then, I can quite understand people going to Ville-d'Avray or Celle-Saint-Cloud or Fontainebleau — no not Fontainebleau, there are too many painters. But I still prefer Paris. Whatever people say, the countryside is for country folk and travelling is for commercial travellers: that's their trade. After a while, it's no joke being stuck in an inn, like a tree left to sprout leaves, in a town where there's nothing but ruins to see. My God, but masters are stupid with their old stones ... as if new, well-tended buildings weren't a hundred times more pleasing to the eye. Quite clearly, Monsieur has absolutely no consideration for me. I may be his servant and my duty may be to serve him, but he does not have the right to make me die of boredom in the Hôtel d'Angleterre. If my dear master — he is, after all, a good master — has encountered some mishap or other, I could only get over it if I found a better job! I'd really like to go and look for him, but which way should I go? Who knows where his fancy has driven him: to the most outlying, impassable spots; into the sorts of death-traps and quagmires he thinks are quaint; he sketches them in his scrapbook, as if there were something special about them. Well, I'll give him three more days to get back; then I'll have news of his disappearance broadcast and stuck up at all the crossroads, as though he were a lost dog. And I'll promise to give a reasonable reward to anyone who returns him.'

Fulfilling his role as the sceptical modern servant, who ridicules the devoted and faithful kind of valet of days gone by, Jack, though a decent man, joked about his worries, which were nevertheless very real. Basically, he liked Guy de Malivert and was attached to him. Although he knew he was written into his master's will to inherit a sum of money that would assure him a life of modest ease, he did not wish him dead.

The landlord was beginning to appear anxious, not about Malivert whose expenses had been paid for but about the two horses he had provided for the expedition. As he was lamenting the dubious well-being of these two incomparable, sure-footed, soft-mouthed creatures that ran with such sweet speed and were driven with a length of silk, Jack grew impatient and said to him with an air of supreme disdain: 'Well, if your two nags have snuffed it, you'll be paid for them.' And this assurance restored the noble Diamantopoulos to his normal state of composure.

The guide's wife was a beautiful, hardy, matronly woman who could have stood in for the caryatid missing from the Pandroison that is now replaced by a terracotta replica. Each evening she came to ask whether Stavros, her husband, had come back with or without the traveller. After the invariably negative response, she went to sit on a stone a little way from the hotel and undid the blonde plaited hairpiece that encircled her dark hair. She shook out her locks and held up her nails to her cheeks as though she wanted to scratch herself. Then she uttered sighs like a ventriloquist and indulged in a theatrical display of grief in accordance with ancient custom. Deep down, she was not really very shaken, for Stavros was a second-rate fellow and quite a drinker. He used to beat her when he was drunk, and did not put much money into the housekeeping although he earned quite a lot by taking foreigners on guided tours. For convention's sake, however, she had to put on a reasonable show of despair. There was no element of slander in the gossip that accused her of finding consolation for her husband's intermittent absences in a handsome wasp-waisted Palikar who wore a bell-bottomed fustanella, made of at least sixty metres of fine pleated cloth, and a red fez with a blue silk tassel that went half way down his back. Her anguish, whether true or false, was expressed in throaty sobs reminiscent of Hecuba's barking, and it annoyed and bothered Jack considerably who, though an unbeliever, was a little superstitious: 'I don't like this woman,' he said 'who howls after her missing husband like a dog that can smell death.' Since the three days he had decided on as the final deadline for Malivert's return had passed, he went to inform the legal authorities.

They undertook the most thorough searches in the probable direction that Malivert and his guide ought to have taken. Every face of the mountain was scoured. And in a sunken lane the carcass of a horse was found lying on its side totally detached from its harness and already half devoured by the crows. A bullet had shattered its shoulder and the animal must have been killed on the spot with its rider. Around the dead creature, the ground seemed to have been trampled as though in a struggle but already too long had passed since the presumed time of the attack, which must have been several weeks earlier. Not much could be inferred from these remains: they had been half destroyed by the rain or the wind. In a mastic tree at the roadside, a branch had been half severed by a passing missile. The upper half had been bent back and it hung down all withered.

The bullet, from a pistol, was found further away in a field. The person who had been attacked seemed to have defended himself. What had been the outcome of the struggle? One had to assume it had been fatal since neither Malivert nor his guide had reappeared. The horse was recognised as one of those rented to the young French traveller by Diamantopoulos. But since more accurate information was not available, the investigation could go no further. All trace of the aggressors and the victim – or victims, for there must have been two of them – was missing. The main path of inquiry was blocked off right from the start. A detailed description of Malivert and Stavros was sent to all possible areas where the road layout could have taken them. They had not been seen anywhere. Their journey had ended there. Perhaps some brigands had taken Malivert off into some inaccessible mountain cave with the idea of holding him to ransom. But this theory collapsed after a few minutes' examination. The bandits would have sent one of their men into the town in disguise and then found a way of getting a letter to Jack containing the terms of the ransom; there would have been a threat of mutilation if there were any delay and death if they were refused. Those are the kinds of dealings that go on in business of this sort. But that is not what had happened. No such piece of paper had come from the mountains to Athens. The brigands' post box had not been used.

Although Jack had not budged from the Hôtel d'Angleterre, he was remarkably perturbed by the idea of returning to France without his master. People might think he had been his murderer. He did not know which saint to turn to and more than ever he cursed the kind of obsession with travel that could lead a decent man to uncivilised areas, where thieves in carnival costumes would shoot at him like a hare.

A few days after those searches, Stavros turned up at the hotel but good God, in what a state! He was haggard, thin, dishevelled and looked wild and crazy, like a spectre that leaves its tomb without shaking off the earth. His sumptuous, quaint costume, on which he prided himself and which had such a good effect on travellers enamoured of local colour, had been removed and replaced by revolting rags all marked with mud from the bivouacs. A greasy sheepskin covered his shoulders and no one would have recognised in him the tourists' favourite guide. His unexpected return was notified to the authorities. Stavros was provisionally arrested for, though he was well-known in Athens and relatively honest,

178

he had, after all, set off with a traveller and come back alone – a turn of events which meticulous legal investigators are not inclined to consider natural. However, Stavros managed to demonstrate his innocence. His work as a guide was logically opposed to his exterminating the travellers from whom he benefited and whom moreover there was no need to murder in order to steal from. Why would he have stayed waiting at the side of the path for victims who followed him quite willingly along the main road and gave him a reasonable share of their gold? But the account he gave of Malivert's death was extremely strange and really was difficult to believe. According to him, they were both riding peacefully along the sunken path at the spot where the horse's carcass was found when a shot from a fire-arm was heard, followed by another a split second later. The first shot had brought down the horse that Monsieur de Malivert was riding and the second hit the traveller himself, who had instinctively moved his hand towards his saddle holsters and let off a pistol shot at random.

Three or four bandits had jumped out of the bushes to rob Malivert. Two others made him, Stavros, get down from his horse and held him by the arms, though he did not attempt any vain resistance.

Until that point, the account had not differed from the normal tales of the highway, but what followed was far less credible, although the guide swore it under solemn oath. He claimed that the face of the dying Malivert, far from conveying any death pangs, radiated instead a celestial bliss, and that next to him he had seen a figure of dazzling whiteness and wondrous beauty who must have been the *Panagia*, and who placed on the traveller's wound, as though to ease his suffering, a hand of light.

The bandits, scared by the apparition, had fled to quite some distance, upon which the beautiful lady had taken the dead man's soul and flown off into the sky with it.

They could never make him alter this statement. The traveller's body had been hidden under a shifted rock at the edge of one of those rivers whose beds are always dry and filled with oleander in summer. As for him, the poor devil, he was not worth killing and so, after stripping him of his beautiful clothes, he was taken a long way into the mountains so that he did not go and report the murder. And it was with great difficulty that he had managed to escape.

Stavros was released. If he had been guilty, it would have been easy for him to reach the islands or the Asiatic coast with Malivert's money. The fact that he came back proved his innocence. The account of Malivert's death was sent to Madame de Marillac, his sister, in roughly the same terms as Stavros had related it. The apparition of Spirite was even mentioned, but as an hallucination conjured up by the guide's fear; his mind did not seem entirely sound.

At about the time when this murder was taking place on Mount Parnassus, the baron de Féroë had retired, as was his wont, to the inaccessible depths of his apartment, and was busy reading that strange and mysterious work by Swedenborg entitled *Marriage in the Other Life*.

As he was reading, he was struck by a strange feeling of unease, as happened when he was being alerted to a revelation. Thoughts of Malivert crossed his mind though they were not brought there by any natural transition. A light spread through the room, its walls became transparent and, like an open-air temple, it was uncovered to reveal a view of immense depth. It was not the sky that arrests the human eye but the sky to which only the eyes of visionaries can penetrate.

At the centre of an effervescence of light, that seemed to issue from the depths of infinity, two spots of an even more marvellous intensity sparkled like diamonds in a flame. They flickered and approached one another and took on the appearance of Malivert and Spirite. They were flying next to one another in a state of heavenly, radiant bliss, caressing each other with the tips of their wings and fondling each other with divinely provocative gestures.

Soon they got closer and closer together and, like two drops of dew rolling around on the same lily leaf, they finally melted into a single droplet.

'There they are ... happy for ever, their souls united to form one angel of love,' said the baron de Féroë with a melancholic sigh. 'So what about me? How much longer will *I* have to wait?'